"Your love," he said against her mouth, "is worth everything."

Anabella studied his hard eyes, his almost arrogant expression. Such a proud, noble face. He could have been a Spanish conquistador, an explorer in search of the New World. Instead he was hers.

"I'll love you forever," she promised.

At first he said nothing. Then his dark eyes grew somber. "You're only seventeen. Forever is an awfully long time."

But his cautious tone made her laugh and she gave her head a shake even as her warm laughter danced between them, a shimmer of exuberance.

"And tell me, Lucio Cruz. When have I ever been afraid of anything?"

by
Jane Porter

The Galván men:
proud Argentinean aristocrats…
who've chosen American rebels as their brides!

Other exciting episodes in this series:

In Dante's Debt #2298
Lazaro's Revenge #2304

Coming Soon

The Spaniard's Passion
December 2004
#2363

Harlequin Presents®:

Intense, international and
provocatively passionate!

Jane Porter

THE LATIN LOVER'S SECRET CHILD

THE Galván Brides

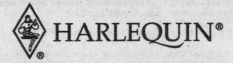
HARLEQUIN®

TORONTO • NEW YORK • LONDON
AMSTERDAM • PARIS • SYDNEY • HAMBURG
STOCKHOLM • ATHENS • TOKYO • MILAN • MADRID
PRAGUE • WARSAW • BUDAPEST • AUCKLAND

ISBN 0-373-12358-2

THE LATIN LOVER'S SECRET CHILD

First North American Publication 2003.

Copyright © 2003 by Jane Porter.

This edition published by arrangement with Harlequin Books S.A.

® and TM are trademarks of the publisher. Trademarks indicated with ® are registered in the United States Patent and Trademark Office, the Canadian Trade Marks Office and in other countries.

Visit us at www.eHarlequin.com

Printed in U.S.A.

PROLOGUE

IT WAS a beautiful afternoon, sunny, cloudless, the sky a pristine blue. Anabella Galván felt the warmth of the sun inside her, her happiness almost as bright.

"Tonight, Lucio, we're going tonight. It's finally happening." She couldn't help smiling. It was impossible to contain her excitement.

"You just like the idea of running away together," Lucio answered, tweaking her nose. "You're such a rebel, Ana."

"Maybe. But I want to be with you and if we worried about what everyone else thought, we'd never be together."

The gaucho nodded his head slowly, his thick black hair loose to his shoulders. He usually wore it tied back but Ana had pulled the leather tie from it moments ago. "You're sure your brother has no idea—"

"Dante's not even at the estancia. He's in Buenos Aires. He's left me with his American, Daisy." Ana's fine black eyebrows arched. "And Daisy is very sweet, but she's far too trusting."

"Your brother's going to be furious."

Ana pressed against Lucio's chest and drew his arms around her. "Stop worrying. Everything's going to be fine."

They were sitting on a stone plaster wall behind the small town center and he dipped his head, kissed her cheek, near her ear. "I just don't want you hurt. I couldn't bear it if anything happened to you."

She laughed at his fears and snuggled closer. "Nothing will happen, Lucio."

They were silent for a moment and the warm breeze ruffled Ana's hair and danced across their skin. Anabella closed her eyes, savoring the afternoon's warmth, the feel of the

5

sun on the top of her head, the strength of Lucio's arms. Everything would be perfect now. She and Lucio together. She and Lucio and the baby. She couldn't forget the baby. The baby made all things possible.

His arms tightened around her. His mouth brushed her ear. "This is crazy, you know," he said, his voice deep.

Ana broke free and turned to face him, her hands supporting her on the rough stone and plaster wall. She studied his face, the black brows, dark eyes, long nose, sensual mouth. He was lovely, but what made him lovely wasn't the symmetry of his features or his imposing size, but rather the beauty on the inside. You could see the fire in his eyes. You could feel his energy. He was so alive. So *real*.

Unlike the people in her world.

Unlike her family.

Anabella swallowed and reaching up lightly traced his temple, his nose, his cheekbone and chin. "I love you, Lucio."

His dark eyes burned hotter, the heat and desire a tangible thing. "Not half as much as I love you."

But his fire didn't scare her. She loved it. She wanted it. He made her feel big and powerful and free. "We'll take the world by storm, Lucio. We'll do it all. See it all. Have it all."

He laughed softly and shook his head. "You're not a dreamer, are you?"

"We *will* have it all," she insisted stubbornly, glaring at him. "We'll have each other. We'll have the baby. What else is there?"

His dark eyes searched hers. She could tell he was amused by her passionate outburst. Little she did upset him. Little she said troubled him. He accepted her for what she was. He accepted her for *who* she was.

"I am poor, Ana," he said slowly, deliberately, his dark gaze intense. "I will never be able to give you—"

"No!" She clapped a hand over his firm mouth, silencing his words. His warm breath tickled her palm but she didn't

remove her hand, unwilling to let him speak the words. "You give me love, Lucio. It's all I've ever wanted, all I've ever needed. Everyone in my family insists on the importance of appearances, propriety, position. You're the only one that just loves me for me."

His fierce expression softened. He drew her hand from his mouth, kissing her palm as he did so. "But *negrita,* I want you to have *everything.*"

She scooted closer to him, inching forward until her thighs pressed his, inching until she'd practically climbed into his lap. "But love *is* everything."

"And our baby?"

"Will be loved." She leaned towards him and touched her lips to the bronze column of his throat. With his Spanish-Indian heritage he tanned easily and she hoped their child would take after him. She wanted the baby to have his dark hair, dark eyes, and golden skin.

"You're determined to have it all, aren't you?" Lucio growled before catching her face in his hands and kissing her deeply.

He drank her in, drank her as if she were air and light and water and Ana felt a shiver of pleasure race beneath her skin. His touch made her feel hot, brilliant, physical.

"Your love," he said against her mouth, "is worth everything."

She held him tightly, pressing her face against his chest. It was such a miracle that they'd found each other. Lucio was a gaucho. She was the daughter of a count. Running off together might be scandalous but it would be the best thing that had ever happened to her.

"You smile," he said, his fingers tangling in her long dark hair.

And she was smiling. "I wish we were leaving now."

"I'll have a horse ready for you later. We'll ride most of the night."

She nodded, the bubble of happiness so big and bright it felt like she'd swallowed the sun itself. She lifted her head to better see his face. "Do you think your family will like me?"

"Without a doubt."

She studied his dark eyes, his almost arrogant expression. Such a proud, noble face. He could have been a Spanish conquistador, an explorer in search of the new world. Instead he was hers.

"I'll love you forever."

At first he said nothing. Then his dark eyes grew somber. "You're only seventeen. Forever is an awfully long time."

But his cautious tone made her laugh and she gave her head a shake even as her warm laughter danced between them, a shimmer of exuberance. "And tell me, Lucio Cruz, when have I been afraid of anything?"

CHAPTER ONE

Five years later...

"ANABELLA, you've been standing at the window all morning. Come sit down. You must be exhausted by now."

Anabella tensed, her eyes so dry and gritty that it hurt to blink. "I can't sit. Not until Lucio comes."

"It could be a while—"

"I don't care," she interrupted huskily, her gaze never leaving the snowcapped Andes. It'd been cold the past few days but this morning was lovely. It felt almost like Spring. "He'll come for me. He promised."

"But we haven't been able to reach him yet, Senora, and you're still weak," the nurse said coaxingly. "You must give us a chance to find him."

Anabella didn't answer. Her hand gripped the gold damask curtain in her hand, fingers trembling. She *was* tired. Her legs felt oddly weak, her muscles fatigued, but she missed Lucio so much. It'd been forever since she last saw him. Yet he would come for her. Lucio never broke his word.

"You've been ill, Senora. You must rest. Conserve your strength." The nurse continued in the same patient voice one would use for a high-strung horse or a difficult child. "At least sit and have your lunch."

"I'm not hungry." Anabella hated how the nurse treated her like a child. Anabella didn't need someone to tell her to rest, to sleep, to eat. She had a brain. She could think for herself.

Not that they were giving her many opportunities to make decisions for herself.

Like coming to this house. She hadn't wanted to be here. The hospital had been bad enough with its antiseptic smells like the cool metallic scent of rubbing alcohol, the pungent disinfectant used to mop the shiny floors, the oddly pleasing odorless hand lotion worn by the staff nurses. But then they brought her to this big mausoleum of a place in the middle of vineyards.

The villa was enormous and formal and stuffed with antiques and fine art. It was a place for grand parties and elegant luncheons and business functions. It was another of Dante's extravagances. He had so many. He was so rich.

Unlike her Lucio.

The only good thing about the house was its proximity to the mountains. And at least from her bedroom window she could see the mountains. Lucio and the mountains were synonymous in her mind. Lucio had grown up in the mountains and his family lived there still.

Her fingers tightened on the silk fabric. "So Dante has called Lucio then?"

The nurse set the clipboard down and her footsteps sounded on the floor. "I don't know. The Count doesn't consult with me." The nurse's hand settled lightly on Ana's shoulder. "Shall we finish getting dressed now? Your brother will be here soon. You don't want to meet him in your nightgown, do you?"

"I don't want to see him."

The nurse withdrew her hand. "You didn't see him yesterday, either."

Ana's stomach knotted. "That's my choice, isn't it?"

"He's your brother—"

"And what business is that of yours, anyway?" Anabella turned from the window, her arms folding across her chest and she stared at the nurse in the trim white dress with the neat white hose and shoes. "And why are you even here? I'm fine. I don't need you. I don't want the fuss."

"I'm sorry. It's your brother's decision."

"And you wonder why I don't want to see him?"

Anabella asked bitterly, moving to a deep armchair in the corner of her room and burying herself inside the protective arms.

Dante, Dante, Dante. It was always about Dante. When Dante said jump, people jumped. But Dante didn't know everything.

Tears stung her eyes and Anabella bent her head, covered her face with her forearm. She felt almost crazy. Her emotions felt so wild, so chaotic and there was a buzz in her head, like the drone of a bee.

"You're not dressed."

Ana stiffened at the sound of the deep male voice. So he'd arrived. She glanced up, her gaze meeting her brother's as he entered her room. He was wearing a charcoal gray suit, a shirt almost the same shade, and no tie. He looked rich, sophisticated, and successful. "I didn't know I had to dress for you."

Count Dante Galván glanced at the nurse and she discreetly slipped from the room. He waited until the door was shut. "What's wrong, Anabella? You're so angry with everyone lately."

Her hands balled into defiant fists. "I want Lucio."

"You don't want him," he corrected sternly. "Trust me, Ana, you don't want—"

"You're wrong!" She slammed her fists on the upholstered arms of the chair. "I do want him. I love him. I miss him—" her voice broke and she shook her head, frustrated, furious, unable to bear Dante's grim expression. He didn't understand. He didn't know what it was like to love someone and yet be denied that person.

"You left him, Anabella." Dante's voice sounded flat. "It was your choice. You realized you didn't have anything in common. You realized you needed something else, something different than what he could provide."

"Stop!" He was making her sick and cold and she longed to take the soft afghan from the foot of the bed and wrap it around her. "You're telling me lies. You're trying to confuse me. But it won't work this time. I know the truth. Lucio *loves* me."

"That's not the point, Ana!"

"It's exactly the point." Her teeth began to chatter. She rubbed her hands along her upper arms trying to get warm, trying to silence the small, frightened voice inside her. Lucio was coming back, wasn't he? He wouldn't leave her here with Dante, would he?

"You're cold." Dante moved forward, lifting the crimson blanket from the bed and covering Ana's shoulders. He tucked the edges of the soft, fuzzy blanket around her before touching her forehead. "You're icy. You need to be resting, Ana. You've worn yourself out."

"I can't rest." Teeth chattering she tipped her head back and looked up at her brother. His face seemed so hard and yet his golden eyes glowed. He might look angry with her but she knew he loved her, and despite all his bullying and strong-arm tactics he wanted what was best for her. "Please Dante, find Lucio. I miss him so much. I can't eat, can't sleep. Please bring Lucio back to me."

There went his wireless phone again.

The small phone clipped to Lucio Cruz's belt silently vibrated yet again, sending tiny currents through his torso. The phone had rung almost constantly during Lucio's three hour meeting with the California Wine Advisory Council and even though he was now on the way to his car, he still hadn't had a moment to check his messages yet.

Lucio reached for his phone as he headed outside to the parking lot where the black convertible Porsche he'd rented at the San Francisco airport waited.

But before he could answer the phone, footsteps sounded on the pavement and Lucio looked up to see Niccolo Dominici, president of the California Wine Advisory Council, approach. Niccolo, owner of Napa's famous Dominici Vineyard, had run the afternoon meeting.

"Come have dinner with us," Niccolo said, sunglasses

on to cut the bright afternoon glare. ''Maggie's just phoned. She's insisting I bring you home with me, wanted me to tell you that you can't say no. She's desperate for adult conversation.''

Lucio's lips tugged. He felt a reluctant smile. Niccolo's wife was beautiful. Spirited. Like his ex-wife Anabella, but unlike Anabella, Niccolo's wife loved him.

His smile faded. ''Thank you for the invitation, but I've work to do—''

Niccolo made an impatient sound. ''You've worked all day. You need dinner. Company. Hotels can be lonely places.''

Actually being in a hotel was less stressful than being home, Lucio thought bitterly. Home didn't feel like home, not anymore. In the divorce settlement Anabella had gotten the house, the upper vineyard, the apartment in Buenos Aires. He'd taken a small place, a new place, in downtown Mendoza. It was a nice apartment in an expensive building. His one bedroom apartment was elegant with excellent light and a magnificent view of the Andes, but he'd left it virtually unfurnished, buying only a table, a chair and a bed.

He didn't need more than that. He didn't intend to be in Mendoza more than he had to. Anabella lived—entertained—in Mendoza. He couldn't bear to be in the vicinity. Too much had happened between them. Too much pain. Too much disillusionment.

Lucio realized Niccolo was watching him, quietly waiting for an answer. ''I'm afraid I wouldn't be good company tonight,'' Lucio answered honestly. ''Besides, you have three little ones at home anxious to see you. They'd rather have you to themselves.''

Lucio had met the children a week ago when he first arrived in California and they were delightful. Jared, the eldest at seven, was fair and wiry with intense blue eyes. Then there was five-year-old Leo, the middle one, the second son, dark like his father with green gold eyes; and the youngest, three-year-old Adriana, with dark curls and dimples and constantly in mischief.

But being with Niccolo, Maggie and the children hadn't been easy. Lucio found himself envious of his colleague, of the life the Italian vintner had made for himself in Northern California. Lucio, too, craved children but Anabella couldn't conceive.

Niccolo's hand suddenly clapped Lucio's shoulder. "You're sure you won't join us?"

"Positive." Lucio started the engine. He just wanted to escape. Niccolo meant well but Lucio couldn't handle the contact, and certainly wasn't up for socializing. It'd taken him a number of years, but he was finally good at growing grapes, crushing fruit and making drinkable dinner wine. He was sticking with his strengths. "Give your wife my best. Tell her we'll have dinner before I go."

Lucio drove fast; taking the narrow winding road from Dominici Vineyard to the highway more quickly than he should—far more quickly than the law allowed—but he'd never followed rules, never believed in rules. Rules, his father used to say were made for the man who couldn't think for himself. Rules, his cowboy culture implied, were for those who needed a norm.

He didn't need a norm.

Even now, despite his success, he didn't want to be part of the norm, or the exclusive society of his aristocratic wife.

Lucio's gaze swept the tight turn ahead and he shifted down, briefly reducing speed until he cleared the turn. The moment he came out of the turn he accelerated hard, practically flying down the stretch of road cutting through the rolling golden hills. Napa was in the middle of an Indian summer and the warm dry air, and the scent of baked earth, ripe fruit, smelled achingly familiar.

Maybe too familiar.

Thankfully this fast, rather reckless, drive was exactly what he needed. Freedom. Space. Speed. Adrenaline.

Racing through the hills reminded him of riding bareback

on a young stallion. Danger heightened the senses and Lucio found himself relishing the rush of dry wind in his face, the hot sun burning down on his head, the ease with which the sports car hugged the turns.

Moving fast, he could almost forget that he'd lost the one person he'd ever loved.

By the time Lucio made it to his hotel room, his phone was ringing again. He answered, hand on the door, half expecting to hear Anabella's brittle, angry voice. A small part of him still hoped she'd phone. A small part of him hadn't accepted reality.

But it wasn't Anabella's voice on the other end of the line. It was Dr. Dominguez, the family physician in Mendoza.

"Where have you been?" Static on the line made the doctor's voice sound unnaturally faint.

Lucio reached for the light switch on the wall. "I've been in meetings."

"I've been calling you, leaving messages—" the connection broke up, and then the doctor's voice came through again, "danger's past—" and faded out only to fade in again, "an immediate return."

Danger? Where was the danger?

It was a terrible connection. Lucio couldn't make out more than a couple words the doctor was saying. He closed the hotel door and headed across the room to see if he couldn't get better reception there. "Stephen, I missed most of what you just said. Can you repeat that, please?"

Dr. Dominguez replied but again it was static once more and Lucio drew back the drapes at the window to let in the light. "I can't understand a word you're saying." Lucio fought to hang on to his temper. "Tell me again. What's wrong? What's happened?"

"Anabella."

"What's happened to Anabella?" Dread seeped through his gut as he pushed open the glass door to the balcony.

But he didn't get an answer. The line went dead.

What the hell? What had happened to Anabella? Lucio swore, gripped his phone and started to punch in Dominguez's number but his phone rang, interrupting him.

In that brief twenty-some seconds of silence his mind had spun a dozen different tragic scenarios.

"What's wrong with Anabella?" Lucio demanded the moment he answered the phone.

The doctor didn't waste time. "We think now it's encephalitis."

"Encephalitis," Lucio repeated, wondering if he'd misheard the doctor. The connection still wasn't the best. What the hell was encephalitis?

"It's a viral infection. It's very rare, almost never heard of in Argentina, which is why we had difficulty with diagnosing the illness. Your wife has been pretty sick, but we think she's out of the woods now—"

"Out of the woods? How sick was she?"

The doctor hesitated, and then cleared his throat. "Encephalitis can be fatal."

"How sick was she?" Lucio repeated with quiet menace.

The doctor didn't reply. Lucio closed his eyes, shook his head, his heart and mind dark.

No one had told him. No one had called him. And it hit him all over again, how he'd always been the outsider. He might have married Anabella, but her family didn't accept him. They'd barely tolerated him and once they knew Ana wanted out of the marriage they did everything in their power to expedite the divorce itself.

No wonder he and Anabella hadn't lasted. They were up against too much. Up against virtually everything.

The doctor cleared his throat again. "As I said, it's not an easy disease to diagnose. It starts out like the flu and quickly progresses. We had to do a lumbar puncture test. A CT brain scan. An MRI scan—"

"Goddamn," Lucio swore, interrupting. A lumbar puncture test? CT scan? MRI scan? They ran all those tests on Anabella without ever calling him...telling him? "When were you going to tell me that my wife might die? After she's already in a coma? When it's time to make the funeral arrangements?''

''She's out of the coma.''

Lucio's hand felt nerveless. *She'd been in a coma?*

''I induced the coma.'' The doctor's voice was calm, reasonable, sounding as if inducing comas were child's play. ''But she came out of it fine, and the coma did exactly what we hoped. The inflammation is gone. We eventually expect a full recovery.''

''You induced a coma.'' Lucio felt a wave of emotion. They'd put her in a coma; placed her in a deep sleep she might never have emerged from and no one—not one person—had given him the chance to say goodbye.

How dare they? How dare the doctors and her family exclude him?

His emotion was nothing short of rage, and hate and a gnawing helplessness. He didn't like being helpless. He didn't accept helpless. Helpless was for those too afraid to act.

He wasn't afraid to act.

But he wasn't free to act.

''Inducing a coma was the best way to limit the seizures. The seizures could have pushed her over the edge.''

Lucio closed his eyes, unable to even bear the vision of Anabella so close to death. She'd been the most important person in his life. He'd loved her more than he'd ever loved anyone and to think he'd almost lost her. Permanently. ''But you've saved her.''

''Yes.'' There was relief in the doctor's voice. ''We have. She's awake, fairly alert.''

''So why are you calling?'' Lucio couldn't hide his bitterness, or the depth of his pain. Once an outsider, always an outsider. To Ana's family he'd always be the gaucho. The peasant. The Indian native. ''Am I to send flowers? Pick up the hospital tab? What's my job now?''

''Help her regain her memory.''

Lucio tensed. It took him a moment to process this. "You said she's recovered."

"Recovering," the doctor corrected. "Her body is stronger, but her mind—" he hesitated, picking his words with care, "—her consciousness is altered, has been altered for quite a while—"

"How long?"

"Three weeks."

Jesus! Lucio rubbed at his temple, his head pounding. He needed sleep. He needed to feel like himself again. "She's been seriously ill for three weeks?"

"Four, actually. Ever since her return from China. But the first week everyone thought it was just the flu. There were headaches, vomiting, the usual."

And then seizures, altered consciousness, coma and loss of memory. Lucio grimly clamped his teeth together to keep from saying something he'd regret.

"She is better now," the doctor reassured. "But she's confused. I think…we all think…she needs you."

She needed *him?*

Lucio nearly laughed out loud. The good doctor didn't know what he was saying. Anabella most certainly did not need him. She'd made that perfectly clear over and over in the past year.

Lucio reached up to pull the black leather tie from his hair. His heavy black hair fell to his shoulders and with a weary hand he rubbed his temple and his scalp. He was tired. Physically, mentally, emotionally.

He couldn't continue like this. Couldn't continue fighting battles he didn't care about. The grapes, the economy, the Argentina export business—these did not move him. They were a duty, an obligation, but were they truly his?

And Ana. She wasn't his anymore, either.

"Not to mince words, but her family hired the divorce attorney. I never thought I'd see them asking me to return."

"I can't speak for Marquita," the doctor replied, referring to Anabella's beautifully preserved mother who had a taste for hard liquor, "but the Count has offered to send his plane."

Lucio almost growled his dislike. "I don't need the Count to send a plane for me. I have transportation of my own, thank you." It was impossible to hide his bitterness. He and Dante were not friends. Would never be friends. He couldn't even bear to be in the same room with Anabella's brother.

The doctor hesitated. "What shall I tell the Count?"

"That I'm packing my things." Lucio drew a deep breath, forcing himself to suppress his anger towards the Galváns. His marriage might be over, but it didn't change his feelings. Married or divorced, in his mind, Anabella would always be his wife. To death do us part, and he'd meant it. "I'll be home tomorrow morning."

But on the plane that night, stretched out in the leather lounge chair in the first class cabin, Lucio's thoughts were tangled. His emotions even more jangled.

He tried to picture Anabella ill. He couldn't. His Ana was tough. Physically, mentally, emotionally. She was as spirited and independent as they came. Nothing touched her. Nothing fazed her.

Ironically, it was her strength that had allowed the divorce to happen in the first place.

She'd been the one who pushed. He'd fought the divorce, fought her, for months, refusing to let go. But his refusal only pushed her further away. Her anger gave way to tears, and then the tears gave way to silence.

They stopped speaking. Stopped being in the same room at the same time. Stopped all communication.

He remembered asking her what she wanted for her birthday and she faced him across the long dinner table, he at one end, she at the other, and she very politely said, "A divorce, please."

And in that calm voice, and that quiet moment, he agreed.

Later when they sat down to sign the papers, he'd hesitated. But tears welled up in her eyes, and she stretched a

hand out across the table, entreating, *Let me go, Lucio.*
We're both so miserable. Please just let me go.

He caught her hands in his and saw the tears in her beautiful eyes, the quiver of her full passionate mouth and felt
hell close round him.

It was over.

Silently he signed his name, dated the document and
walked away without another word.

But he hadn't really walked away, he thought now, leaning his head back against the wide leather seat. He'd been
ignoring the truth, denying the truth, unable to handle the
fact that Ana could so easily dispose of him, of them.

Eyes burning, Lucio swallowed the rush of hurt.

You were wrong, Anabella, he thought, eyes closed, chest
livid with pain. *I might have been miserable at times, but I
never wanted out. Your love might have died. But I will
always love you.*

The commercial jet landed in Chile early the next morning, where Lucio took a connecting flight, arriving in
Mendoza just after ten. A car was waiting for him, and the
driver—one of Lucio's own—didn't offer any information
and Lucio didn't ask.

Mendoza had only been home for four years. Lucio had
bought the vineyard, villa and business with one cashier's
check. He'd known nothing about the winery business at the
time. He just knew it was respectable and respectable was
what Ana's family demanded.

But now as the chauffeur wove on and off the highway
towards the villa nestled in the foothills, Lucio couldn't help
reflecting that Ana had loved the gaucho, not the vintner.

The black town car drove through ornate iron gates tipped
in gold, and turned down a long private lane leading to an
elegant two-story villa, the smooth plaster walls a wash of
soft apricot paint. It might be wine country Argentina, but
the house was all Tuscany. The original owners had been
Italian. The wood beams, hardwood floor, roof tiles all imported from Italy.

With the morning sun casting a warm rosy glow across the front of the one-hundred-year-old villa with the tall cypress trees and the plaster arch flanking the front door, the house looked magical.

Lucio felt a pang of loss. This is the place he'd brought Ana as his new bride. This is the place he'd thought they'd finally make their home.

Nothing ever worked out as one hoped, did it?

"Shall I bring your bags in, Senor?" The chauffeur's respectful voice interrupted Lucio's painful thoughts.

Lucio shook off his dark mood, stepped from the car, and adjusted the collar on his black leather traveling coat. He'd do what he'd have to do. "No, Renaldo. I'll be staying at my apartment downtown."

Suddenly there was a shout from upstairs. He heard his name called. Once, twice, and Lucio turned to look up at the second floor of the villa. The windows were open to welcome the freshness of the morning. He searched the windows for a glimpse of Anabella but saw nothing.

Seconds later the front door burst open and suddenly she was there, on the doorstep, breathless from the dash down the stairs.

"Lucio," Anabella cried, green eyes bright. "You're home!"

CHAPTER TWO

FOR a long moment Lucio could think of nothing to say. It felt as if his brain had stopped functioning altogether and he simply stared at Anabella, amazed to see her downstairs, at the door.

The doctor had made her sound ill—fragile—but she practically glowed, her skin luminous and her green eyes bright like Colombian emeralds. "Are you all right?" he asked.

She was barefoot and wearing snug jeans, a crisp white blouse, and her long glossy black hair hung loose. "Now that you're here."

Now that you're here.

Her soft, husky voice burrowed deep inside his heart. She sounded so glad to see him, so unlike the Anabella he'd last seen eight weeks ago, just hours before she left on her big shopping trip to Asia.

That Anabella, the antiques buyer, had been dressed immaculately in a black suit, high black heels, her red leather suitcases stacked at the door.

She'd stood on the doorstep of the villa for a long silent moment looking at him before smiling faintly. "Well, this is it," she said, her cool smile not reaching her intense green eyes.

"Is it?"

Her head tipped, giving him a flash of her black hair smoothed into a sophisticated French twist. "I think so."

"And you get to make all the decisions?" He shot back, regretting that he'd driven to the house to say goodbye, regretting that he couldn't even contain his temper.

He knew she hated his temper. She hated the unresolved

issues still simmering between them. Her cool smile slowly faded. "No, Lucio, I didn't make all the decisions. *We* made them together." And pulling on her black leather traveling gloves, she headed for her car, her head high, her slender back straight.

And that's how he'd remembered her. Cool, elegant, an ice maiden. But that wasn't the woman before him now.

"Where have you been, Lucio?" Ana's voice sounded uncertain and her unblinking eyes held his.

"On a trip."

Her uncertain smile faded, as did some of the joy from her eyes. "You said you'd never leave me."

He frowned, puzzled. "We agreed—"

"To be together," she interrupted fiercely, finishing the sentence for him. And her expression darkened for a moment before she struggled to smile once more. Lucio could feel her struggle. She was trying to make it light between them but on the inside she was hurt. Angry.

"I'm here now," he answered, unable to think of anything else to say even as his mind raced. She'd been the one to send him away, but that didn't matter now. He could see that Ana was confused and he felt the urge to protect her, shield her, from memories that hurt. "Everything will be fine now."

But her eyes filled with tears and she looked away, biting her lip. "It's too late," she said sadly.

"What's too late?"

She hunched her shoulders and her body quivered. "They've done terrible things, Lucio. Things I can't even tell you."

His heart faltered. And then he remembered the doctor's caution, the warning that Ana wasn't herself, and that her memory wasn't what it'd once been.

She must be talking about the illness, he reassured himself. No one had harmed her. He might not like her family, but they loved Ana. Dante loved Ana.

"Of course you can tell me," he said gently. "You tell

me everything. You always have." *Once,* he silently corrected. *Once you told me everything. Once we were as close as two people could be.* But that was long ago and it'd been years since they were so open, so free, so hungry together.

"You told me to wait at the café. I waited and waited but you never came. What happened? I was so afraid and then my mother's people came and they brought me home."

He didn't know what to say.

There was only one time when they were separated, forcibly separated, and that was years ago. That episode was the darkest point in his life, the point where all seemed lost.

She took a step away and her hands went to the pockets of her jeans. "Do you know what it's like to be left? To be abandoned in the middle of the night?" Her rigid shoulders drew her white cotton blouse taut. She still had such a beautiful body, her breasts round and full, her torso lean, her hips curved beneath the faded denim. "I felt so lost, so confused. And I've been waiting for you ever since. Waiting for you to come find me again."

But he had found her again. He'd found her three and a half years ago and they'd moved here, and later married, but their happiness hadn't lasted. It hadn't worked the first time. And it hadn't worked the second, either. Their passion, their attraction couldn't handle the brunt of reality.

Yet that was all water under the bridge. Clearly she didn't remember anything since that terrible night five years ago.

"You said you'd be there for me," she whispered, eyes blazing now, furious. Accusing. "You lied to me. You weren't there when I needed you most."

"I'm here now."

Her brilliant green gaze held his, and she searched his eyes, her full lips pressed into a mutinous line. He didn't know what she was searching for. He didn't know what she hoped to find.

"Are you going to stay?" she asked at length.

The air felt bottled in his lungs. "As long as you want me to stay."

"I want you to stay forever."

The innocence of her answer, the childlike honesty, made him ache. His chest burned, his heart felt as if it were on fire. She was torturing him.

She'd been the one to send him away, he heard a voice protest inside his head. She'd been the one that wanted the divorce. Insisted on the divorce.

But that didn't matter now, he silently argued. Right now she needed him. And that was all that mattered.

She grabbed the lapel of his leather coat between her hands. "Look at me," she commanded, staring up into his face, her eyes almost feverishly bright. "Look me in the eye and promise me that you'll stay."

He leaned over, kissed the top of her glossy head. "I'm staying, Ana." He whispered the words in her ear. "I promise."

Lucio became conscious that they were still standing on the front steps of the villa with Renaldo. A woman in a white uniform hovered on the other side of the door. Everything was so public, he thought. Nothing was ever private anymore.

"Now can I come in, Ana?" he asked, tipping her chin up, forcing her to meet his gaze. "Will you let me come inside, and take my coat off, and just be with you?"

Ana's heart melted at the warm intensity in Lucio's dark eyes. This was the way he used to look at her, this was the way he used to love her. With so much passion. And so much conviction. This was the Lucio who was going to take her away.

"Yes." She slid her hands into his, happiest when touching him. "Come inside, but I warn you, this place is just the kind of house you hate."

"It's not so bad," he answered, his voice almost strangled.

She saw his mouth tighten. She knew he preferred simple things and this villa was typical of the Galván's aristocratic lifestyle. "It is. It's pretentious. Packed with antiques and knickknacks and expensive art. But we don't have to stay here much longer.''

He let her lead him through the long entry. ''And where would we go?''

Ana wanted to shrug, answer something light and frivolous. But she didn't feel light on the inside. She felt wild, driven. *Obsessed.*

''Ana?'' he gently prompted.

She balled her hands into fists. ''I want him back. I need him back.'' Her voice dropped. ''Oh Lucio, I have to get him back.''

Lucio's brow furrowed. His dark eyes met hers. ''Who, Ana? Who are you talking about?''

''The baby.''

''What baby?''

She pressed her fists to her chest, trying to contain her fear. ''*Our* baby.''

Gingerly he reached out to touch her cheek. ''Ana, there is no baby. You miscarried.''

''I didn't.''

''You did. We don't have children.''

She hated the rush of wild emotion. ''We do. We have a boy.''

''*Negrita*, listen to me—''

''How can you not remember?'' She searched his face, searched for a sign, some light, a hint of recognition. ''Lucio, what's wrong with you? You have to find our baby. You have to rescue our baby.''

Lucio couldn't answer. He didn't know how. His hand fell from her face.

It was worse than the doctor had said, he thought. Far worse. The doctor had said prepare yourself, but how to prepare oneself for this?

Lucio swallowed the lump filling his throat, struggling to come to grips with the shock. This wasn't Anabella. This couldn't be Anabella.

And then she whimpered softly. ''Could we sit down?''

she asked, her voice growing hoarse. "Somewhere dark, please."

He immediately reached for her. "Your head hurts." He lightly touched her forehead with his fingertips. She felt cool and yet just the touch of his fingers to her temple made her wince.

He glanced up, saw that the nurse had quietly materialized. "The nurse is here—"

"I'm fine. Really. I just need to sit." But she was flinching at the sound of her own voice and her shoulders arched, rising towards her ears.

Lucio couldn't bear for her to suffer, and she was suffering. He took her hand in his. Her pain was like a live thing and it spread through her hot and consuming. He felt it in her skin, in her pulse, in her mind.

He swung her into his arms and carried her up the stairs to her bedroom. "There must be something they can do, something they can give you," he said, carrying her to her bed and setting her down on top of the burgundy silk coverlet.

Ana rolled over onto her side. "I don't want anything." She looked up at him and her eyes were dark. "The medicine makes me sleepy, and I can't sleep right now. I have to think—"

"How can you think when your head hurts so bad?"

"But I have to. I have to get ready to go for him."

Him. Not this crazy mumbo jumbo again. Lucio suppressed a sigh, feeling as if he'd stepped into a dense fog. But he had to find his way clear. He had to find a way to help her.

Crossing the floor, Lucio went to the window and drew the drapes to cut the glare. "Better?" he asked as the spacious bedroom darkened.

"Much." She managed a small smile but he felt how her body seemed to shimmer with a ceaseless, restless energy.

He returned to her side and sat down, next to her on the bed. She pressed her face to his thigh, her hand covering his knee. "Stay," she whispered, sagging against him, part fatigue, part relief.

"Of course."

"And you're not angry?"

She was so tired, he thought. The wild horse had nearly trampled her down. He smiled at her a little, still calming, reassuring. "Why would I be angry? You've done nothing wrong."

"But the baby—" She broke off, shook her head and looked at him with fear, with need, with painful vulnerability, but there was something else in her eyes now. Trust.

It was as if the last five years had fallen away and she was a child again, the seventeen-year-old he'd met who craved love.

He stroked her long hair back from her face. "I would never be upset with you about losing the baby. I promise, Ana."

Grateful tears burned her eyes and she nestled closer, feeling his warmth, letting his heat creep into her. "I can't believe you're really here," she whispered. She carried his hand to her cheek, and held it as if it were a life preserver in the middle of the sea. "It's like a dream."

He sat with her until she slept, and once he was sure she was peacefully sleeping, he headed to the door but once there, he couldn't make himself leave. He stood in the doorway of her darkened room and looked at her where she lay curled on her side.

He could just make out her profile in the dim light. Her face was as perfect as it ever had been—fine, straight nose, slightly turned up at the end, full mouth, firm chin, high cheekbones and wide brow—but it wasn't her beauty that moved him. It was just being back here, being so close to her again and after all these months, after all this time when he'd thought he was reconciled to living without her, he found himself burning with emotion.

Burning with need.

What the hell had happened to them? Where had everything gone wrong?

Suddenly Lucio resented Ana's illness and helplessness, resented the fact that she didn't remember—couldn't remember—while he felt everything.

He felt the anger, the guilt, the sense of betrayal. He felt loss and grief and rage because dammit, he'd wanted this to work. He'd given everything to their relationship and why hadn't it been right?

Worst of all, he still missed her so much. *Physically* missed her. He missed holding her, feeling the shape and weight of her, missed her softness against his body. And it hurt, too, that she'd been the one to say *enough,* to say she'd had all she wanted, all she needed, and now she was ready to move on with the rest of her life.

What was the rest of her life?

What was his?

Shaking his head, he left her room and quietly closed the door behind him. The nurse was seated in a chair outside Anabella's room and she looked up at him as he passed. "Everything okay?" she asked.

Lucio nodded. "She's asleep."

His eyes felt gritty as he descended the staircase and blinking, he pushed back the sadness, pushed back the ambivalent emotions. This wasn't the time, he told himself. And this most certainly wasn't the place.

Seated in Ana's office, Lucio sorted through her mail, filed the stacks of paperwork, wrote checks for businesses that had sent them statements. He'd forgotten how large her business had grown. She owned a shop in Buenos Aires and another here in Mendoza. The Mendoza store was newer. It didn't have the business Anabella had hoped for. He studied her accounts for a moment, knowing she'd stretched herself too thin, taken on too much. She'd wanted to be successful, wanted to prove to everyone she wasn't the baby of the family anymore, but the sophisticated antique dealer. The *expert.*

He smiled a little and leaning forward he picked up a slender cloisonné clock from the corner of her desk. He'd never seen the clock before. It was turquoise blue with a round ivory face and a pendulum of gold in the shape of a sunburst.

There was a knock on the door and the door opened. The housekeeper quietly carried a tray into the office with a late lunch and placed it on the edge of Lucio's desk. "I know you haven't eaten anything since you arrived," Maria, the housekeeper said, pushing the tray towards him a little.

"I'm not hungry," he answered, replacing the clock back on Anabella's desk.

The housekeeper glanced at the clock. "The Senora brought it back from her last trip."

The trip from China. Lucio felt an urge to throw the clock, break it in a thousand pieces. If Anabella hadn't been chasing all over the world in search of exotic antiques she'd be well now.

He glanced up at Maria. She was a slim barely graying woman in her fifties. He mustered a smile. "How are you?"

"I'm fine, Senor." She'd been hired after Lucio and Anabella married. Anabella had hired her. "But you are missed."

How nice to hear something like that, especially after the past six months when he felt completely dispensable. "Thank you."

"Will you be here long?" the housekeeper asked.

Would he be here long? Yes. No. Only as long as Anabella needed his help.

Only until she sent him away again.

Wearily, Lucio leaned back, rubbed his eyes. "It depends."

"Your room has been made up."

The room he'd been banished to when Anabella stopped wanting him in her bed. "Thank you." He watched the housekeeper start to leave and he sat forward. "Maria—"

She turned towards him. "*Sí,* Senor?"

How odd that he already felt like such an outsider. It'd only been a couple months since he moved out of the villa. "Let me know what I can do to help you and the rest of the staff. I realize things are not...normal."

Maria bowed her head. "But what is normal, Senor? I don't think there is a normal. I think there is just life."

Lucio was still in the office two hours later when Maria knocked on the door again. He'd dozed off in the chair, slumped back, and he woke with a start. "Yes?" he called gruffly, pushing himself forward, and rubbing the sleep from his eyes. He'd slept hard and he shook his head a couple times, finding it difficult to wake.

"The Count Galván is here," Maria said entering the room and taking the empty tray from a side table. "He's waiting for you in the salon."

Lucio passed a hand across his face once again. So the big brother had arrived. Dante Galván certainly didn't waste time.

Lucio was tempted to have Maria show the Count into the study, but glancing around the study with the framed pictures of Anabella on the desk and the personal keepsakes on the bookshelves made the room feel far too intimate.

Better to meet on neutral ground.

Or as neutral a ground as they were going to find in Lucio's former house.

Entering the salon Lucio found his brother-in-law standing in the great room with the high painted beams, the plaster walls washed cream, the floor terra-cotta tiles imported from Italy. The oil paintings all dated from the 17th Century and the rich art and fine antiques spoke of wealth, class, prestige.

Lucio saw Dante glance around the room, Dante's gaze briefly settling on one of the Italian paintings, a landscape with cherubs and maidens frolicking at a tree-shaded lake.

"You know how valuable these are, don't you?" Dante said, gesturing to the wall. "Especially this one," he added, pointing to the maidens by the lake.

Lucio would have smiled if he had the strength. With his world coming down around him, Dante wanted to discuss Lucio's wealth? "Yes."

Dante continued to study the oversize canvas. "When did you buy it?"

"Before I married your sister." Meaning, with my money, not hers. And not yours.

Dante's head lifted and the two men, both Argentine, Dante Italian aristocrat, and Lucio, Spanish-Indian, stared at each other with open hostility.

"I bought the house complete." Lucio broke the tension-fraught silence. "The owner fell on hard times. I bought the land, the villa and all the furnishings with cash."

Dante's lashes flickered down but Lucio saw the doubt in his eyes. "You've never explained how you made your money."

"I made my fortune gambling—"

"Gambling?"

"And then took what I made at the gaming tables and invested it here," Lucio concluded as if Dante had never interrupted.

Dante made a rough sound. "Gambler to vintner? Sounds awfully far-fetched."

"I don't owe you an explanation, Count. But I've always been a gambler. You should know that. I wouldn't be here now if I didn't take risks."

"You mean, you wouldn't have seduced my sister—"

"No." Lucio felt his temper rise but he kept it controlled, hidden by a pleasant smile. "I wouldn't be here now, this afternoon, if I didn't believe that this was a good opportunity for both of us."

"Opportunity?" Dante shot him a sharp glance. "You don't honestly think you've got a chance with her again?"

Lucio shrugged. "What can I say? I'm an optimist. I will never give up on Anabella. I will never give up on us." And Lucio had said the words to spite the Count, but once he'd spoken the words he realized he meant them. He did want a second chance. Maybe God had given him a second chance to make Ana fall in love with him again.

Dante's eyes narrowed and his expression grew bitter. He moved towards the window and stared out, his gaze fixed on the dark green vineyards undulating in the distance.

For a long moment Lucio said nothing. He just watched Dante and waited for whatever was to come next. Lucio could afford to wait. It's all he'd been doing for weeks. Months.

Years.

Finally Dante turned, acknowledged Lucio with a slight nod of his head. "I suppose I should thank you for coming."

Lucio bit his tongue.

"The doctor said you were in California," Dante continued.

"You waited an awfully long time to call."

"I waited until Ana asked for you." Dante's golden gaze clashed with Lucio's. "I wouldn't have called you otherwise."

Lucio kept his temper—just barely. And yet he had to keep reminding himself not to pick a fight with his brother-in-law. Feuding wouldn't help Anabella. What he needed was facts. More information. Pieces of the missing puzzle. "Is this how she emerged from the coma?"

"She was hallucinating even before your Dr. Dominguez induced the coma. It was the hallucinations that helped get her properly diagnosed. Until then everyone here, including her staff, believed she had the flu."

"You visited her here then?"

"Your housekeeper called me and I flew out. I sent for the ambulance as soon as I arrived. I knew it was serious. She was feverish. She was definitely ill."

"And that was what? A month ago?" Despite his best intentions, Lucio felt the bitterness rise. He wanted to remain calm, controlled, but deep down he'd never forgive Dante for shutting him out.

"Nearly." Dante hesitated for a long moment. He appeared at a loss for words. "She is better," he said quietly. "She may not be the old Anabella yet, but she's greatly improved from where she was a week ago."

Lucio could feel the Count's concern. Dante genuinely cared for Anabella and Lucio was reminded of the autumn five years ago when he first met Ana and her family. Just seventeen, she was starting her last year of school, and already such a rebel, so at odds with her older brother's authority.

Dante and Anabella. The two had gone round and round but no matter what happened between them, they were family.

Lucio slowly exhaled, the air almost hissing between his lips. "I'm curious about your definition of better."

The Count looked at him, puzzled. "Her muscle tone is returning. Her strength is returning, but as you might have noticed, there are some memory issues."

Lucio didn't know whether to laugh or cry. "Oh, I noticed."

There was a moment of silence following Lucio's answer and as the silence lengthened the Count's expression grew wary. "What happened? How did she react to you when you arrived—"

Dante was interrupted by a scream from upstairs, the shout carrying down the stone stairwell into the high ceilinged living room. Dante jerked but Lucio's features remained hard, impassive. In the six hours he'd been home, he'd heard every sound imaginable.

"What the hell was that?" Dante demanded, his gaze lifting to the ceiling where the beams had been stenciled in cream, red and green designs.

Lucio moved swiftly towards the stairs. "Anabella."

CHAPTER THREE

THE furious cry was followed by the sound of bare feet running down the stairs. Anabella practically jumped down the last two stairs, her white shirt untucked, her long hair flying. "What do you want, Dante? What are you planning now?"

Dante took a stunned step backwards, hands rising to calm his youngest sister. "I came to see you."

"And do what?" Her fine aristocratic features were pinched and her dark-lashed eyes bright. She reached up and swiftly knotted her hair into a rough ponytail. "Or do you not think I know what you want to do, what you intend to do?"

His expression hardened. "I have no intentions," he said impatiently. "I'm here because you've been sick and I've been worried."

Ana made an indignant sound and her hands flew in quick Italian gestures. "I haven't been sick. I've just been upset. I missed Lucio, but he's back now." She drew a quick breath, eyes blazing even hotter. "And no one can keep us apart now. *No one,* Dante. Not you. Not Mama. Not even all of Mama's hired soldiers."

"You're being irrational, Ana. I have no desire to keep you apart—"

"Liar!"

The color drained from Dante's face. *"Ana."*

Brilliant tears filled her eyes. "Don't say my name like that. Don't say anything to me at all. Ever since Tadeo died you've tried to control me. You're so scared that I'll turn into Tadeo—but I'm not Tadeo! I don't do drugs. I don't drink. I just love Lucio. But even that makes you crazy."

"No, Ana."

"*Yes*, Dante. *Yes*." She jabbed his chest with the tip of her finger. "You and Mama. Always interfering. Never able to leave me alone." She broke off, eyes filling with tears, and she looked at him, hurt, confused, angry. "Why can't I want something different from the rest of you?"

Dante said nothing and the two stared at each other as if enemies instead of brother and sister.

She was living in the past. She'd forgotten that she and Dante were the best of friends, forgotten that it was Dante she confided in now.

"If you don't go, Dante, I will." Anabella threw back her head and swiftly wiped a tear from her eyes. "I don't want to be in the same place with you."

Dante looked helplessly at Lucio. "*Por Dios.* She's lost her mind!"

"This isn't the Anabella you saw a week ago, was it?" Lucio asked grimly.

"*No.*"

"Well, it's the one I came home to this morning."

Anabella grabbed Lucio's arm. "Don't talk to him. Have nothing to do with him. He's not to be trusted."

"It's okay, Ana."

"No, it's not. He's going to get rid of you. He's going to do something to make sure you stay away—"

"Ssssh, *chica*," Lucio interrupted soothingly. He cupped her cheek, stroked the warm softness. "It's all right. You go upstairs. Wait for me. I'll handle this."

Anabella still clung to his arm. "And you won't leave me?"

"No. I promise."

Reassured, Anabella climbed the stairs but then pausing halfway, leaned over the banister to shoot her brother a contemptuous glance. "I know you," she challenged Dante. "I know how you think."

Lucio had had enough. He headed up the stairs and swung

Anabella into his arms. He couldn't handle much more of this today.

"Let's run away," she whispered, wrapping her arms around his neck, her breath warm against his skin. "Let's leave tonight. When the others are asleep."

He said nothing. He let her keep talking as he finished climbing the stairs. The world she lived in right now confounded him. Where was she? What was going on in her head?

"They'll hurt you, Lucio," Ana said, her hands tightening around his neck. "I heard them talking. They want to keep us apart. They want to make sure we'll never be together again. Whatever you do, don't trust Dante. He's not your friend. He won't be fair with you."

Lucio gritted his teeth, wanting her to be quiet, wanting her to stop with all this chatter. These nonsensical words were like a hammer to his brain. She was dredging up old memories, wretched memories, memories of the night when he'd been beaten so badly that it had been weeks before his broken bones healed, months before he could stand properly.

"Ana, no one can take you from me," he said gruffly, walking through her bedroom to the ensuite bath. He placed her in the center of the black marble counter. "We're together now. You belong with me."

"Dante doesn't think so!" She scooted backwards on the counter until her back bumped the mirrored wall and she stared up at him, eyes dark with anger, her black lashes still matted with tears. "Dante will never accept that I've a mind of my own...that I'm capable of making decisions on my own."

She looked so small on the counter, and yet so feisty. A caged jaguar.

He reached up to lightly touch her temple. How much did he remember? How much did she know? "Ana—where are you?"

Her dark green eyes shone with fresh tears. Her hands fluttered in his. "I am here, Lucio."

This was bizarre, he thought. It was like being in a science fiction movie. He was living two lives at one time—the one before and the one right now and it was the oddest, most uncomfortable sensation. "You don't need to fear Dante," he said slowly. "And you don't need to worry about me. I'm not as naive as I used to be."

She slid forward on the counter and wrapped her legs around him, almost catlike in her grace. Lightly she ran her hand up his thigh. "He'll try to pay you off. He'll give you anything you want because he wants to keep you away from me."

Lucio tensed as her fingers trailed across the taut muscle of his thigh. She was stirring his body and he grew hard at the light, teasing touch.

"That's all in the past," he said, trying to remove her hand from his leg without hurting her. It was one thing to return home and provide some stability. It was another to pretend they were still…intimate.

But she wouldn't move her hand and she raked her nails against his dark trousers, her nails sharp enough to make him feel their hard edge through the stiff fabric. "But you do believe me?"

"Yes."

"Good. Because if you don't, I'd have to punish you." And her tone lightened, becoming almost teasing and she was smiling at him, smiling playfully, happily, the way she once had all those years ago when they used to have so much fun together. "Maybe I'll punish you anyway."

Her teasing tone, the rake of her nails against his thigh made him ache. It'd been so long since they'd made love. And Anabella was the only woman he wanted in his bed. Anabella was the only woman he'd ever wanted period.

"Those delights will have to wait," he answered, fighting the urge to touch her, fighting the need to draw closer, to part her thighs and press against her.

He shouldn't be surprised she could still make him feel so much. She was impossible. Incorrigible. No one stood a chance resisting Anabella. He'd never wanted to resist her before. "How does your head feel?"

"Better. Headache's all gone." And she raked her nails across his butt before tucking her fingers into his belt loops. "See, all I needed was you to find me. Be with me. We belong together."

Studying her clear bright eyes, her olive complexion with just a hint of dusty pink in the cheeks, he silently agreed with her. Yes, they did belong together and suddenly Lucio desperately wanted to make everything the way it once was, the way it had been between them when they wanted nothing but each other. Life had been so simple then. Life had made such perfect sense.

"Why don't you take a shower and dress for dinner," he said, resisting the desire to put his hand on her hip, resisting her sweetly tempting curves.

She leaned against him, her breasts brushing his chest and grinned. "Yes. Dinner. Sounds wonderful. I'm starving."

But from the wicked gleam in her eyes he knew she wasn't just asking for steak and fries.

His body grew hotter, harder, the softness of her breasts imprinted on his chest.

"Great. I haven't had much today, either." His voice sounded hoarse. He felt utterly exhausted. Resisting Anabella was going to kill him. "You shower. Dress. Take your time. Then we'll have a nice meal together downstairs."

He leaned forward to kiss her temple but Ana wrapped an arm around his shoulders, and slid forward yet again, bringing her in full contact against his groin. He inhaled sharply as he felt her everywhere—her full soft breasts, the warmth of her thighs where they wrapped around his hips, the slender shape of her pressed against him.

She looked up at him, her green eyes vivid and with one hand she reached for his thick, tightly bound ponytail low at his nape. He felt her fingers slide through his hair and then the cool brush of fingertips against his neck. Her light knowing touch shot a ball of fire through his groin. He was already hard but he felt close to exploding now.

"Do not," she whispered fiercely even as her green eyes sparkled with humor and mischief, "kiss me as if you are my grandmother."

Lucio choked on a laugh. He brushed his lips across her forehead before firmly pushing her away and taking a step back.

She sat tall on the counter. "You'll pay for that."

He laughed again. He couldn't help it. This was so Anabella, so perfectly like his Anabella that he couldn't help the great wave of relief riding through him. Anabella would recover. Anabella would be herself. "Can't wait," he replied before he turned away and headed downstairs.

Dante hadn't gone. He was pacing the living room as Lucio descended the stairs.

"She's mad," Dante said, meeting Lucio at the bottom of the stairs. "She's lost her mind."

"She's not crazy," Lucio answered almost cheerfully, tying his hair back again. His body hummed, and he felt hot, hungry and more than a little relieved. He was only just beginning to understand. It had taken him a while, but it was starting to add up, starting to come together.

She hadn't lost her mind. She'd lost her memory.

"Anabella has gone back in time," Lucio said, mentally sorting through his observations, piecing together all the conversations he'd had with her since returning. "And she seems to be living in the past right now."

Dante looked even more appalled. "She's back in time? But where? When?"

"That I haven't figured out yet."

"But you do think she's gone back a number of years?"

"Well, certainly back to a place where she felt you were oppressive—"

"I was never oppressive!"

Lucio laughed without the least bit of humor. Dante was kidding himself. "You sent the police after us. Your mother's hired guns nearly killed me."

"My mother just wanted Anabella home."

"Enough said."

Dante sighed, ruffled the back of his hair, clearly at a loss. None of this was easy. None of this made sense. "So you really don't think she's gone over the edge?"

"No. She just needs time and a little less pressure. And frankly, I think your visits are harming her more than they're helping. You need to give her space. She needs to recover at her own pace."

"I think her doctor can be the judge of that."

"You forget, her doctor works for me, Dante. Ana might be your sister, but she's *my* wife."

Dante's dark head jerked up. "Your wife? She's divorced you!"

"The divorce isn't final."

"But legally—"

"Legally she's still my wife."

The two men stared at each other for a long unending moment before Dante gave his head a bitter shake. "So you're back in charge, are you?"

Lucio hated the violence of his emotions, hated that he wanted to grab Dante and do bodily harm to him. He inhaled deeply, held his breath, fighting for control.

Slowly he exhaled. He had to stay calm. It wouldn't be fair to Anabella to get into a shouting match with her brother now. She was just upstairs and it'd be far too easy for her to overhear things she wasn't ready to hear.

"I don't like this any more than you do, Dante. This isn't easy for me. I never wanted the divorce. That was her decision, her doing. And she might not remember the present, but I do. I know her feelings changed for me. I know how miserable she was with me."

Dante's narrowed glance met Lucio's. "Yet she doesn't remember any of that now."

"She will."

"And until then? From what I saw here, Anabella still imagines the two of you wildly in love."

Lucio's hard smile faded. "Then I guess I'll have to play along."

Dante's lashes flickered, concealing his expression. "And you can do this? You can stay here and put yourself in the middle of her drama?"

"I don't have a choice."

"Of course you have a choice! You have another home, another life. You could be there instead of here." The Count turned away, passed a hand over his eyes. "You hope to use her illness to your advantage. You're going to try to win her back."

"And is that such a crime?"

Dante's head lifted and his cynical gaze clashed with Lucio's. Lucio didn't blink. He'd pledged himself to Anabella five years ago, three years before they married. His love had nothing to do with a ceremony and a piece of paper.

He loved Anabella simply because she existed.

"She's never been happy living with you," Dante said at last. "It's the idea of you she loves. Not the reality."

It's the idea she loves. Not the reality. The words repeated in Lucio's brain. He held still, flinching inwardly as the words sank in.

Dante's assessment was harsh, sharp, and his words wounded. But Lucio kept the hurt from his expression. "I will call you with updates," he said evenly. He wouldn't say more than he already had. "I promise to phone the moment she begins to improve."

"But otherwise you're telling me to stay home?"

Lucio managed the briefest of smiles. "I'm asking you to give Ana time."

After Dante left, Lucio stepped into the kitchen and requested that dinner be served in the small study downstairs instead of carried to Anabella's room. Then Lucio headed upstairs to check on his wife.

"He's gone?" Anabella asked hopefully as Lucio entered the room. She was sitting on the foot of her bed, wrapped up in a thick bath towel, her wet hair slicked back from her beautiful face.

Lucio felt a craving to touch her, and he suppressed the craving just as quickly as it flared. "He's returning to Buenos Aires. He's going home and back to work."

"Good. I don't like him!"

"Ana, you adore him." He stared down at her, arms folded over his chest and for a moment he wondered what he'd gotten himself into. What if she never did improve? What if she never regained her memories? Never regained her independence? What then?

But Lucio wouldn't think that far. No reason to go there yet. He reminded himself that she was young and strong and intelligent. Of course she'd improve. They'd just have to take it slowly. They'd have to be patient.

"Dinner's ready," he said, trying hard to make it sound as if everything was normal, that everything would eventually be normal. "Except you're still wearing a towel."

"You don't think it's romantic?"

"Not unless you're the matching bath mat."

He was rewarded with a laugh. Grinning, Ana slid off the edge of the bed. "Actually, I did want to dress but I couldn't find my clothes. Do you know where Dante put my suitcase?"

Lucio cocked his head a little. Was she serious? "They're in your closet, Ana."

"Where's my closet?"

"There. In your room."

"Show me."

He walked her to the massive walk-in closet across from her en suite bath. Flicking on the closet light he gestured to the rods of hanging clothes and the long wall lined with shoe boxes. "This is your closet."

Ana peered in. Her brow furrowed as she scanned the racks of suits, dresses, long evening gowns. "Very funny. Now where are *my* clothes? My shirts, my shoes, my jeans?"

It hit him all over again.

She didn't *know*. She didn't recognize anything here, didn't realize that she wasn't Anabella the teenager but Anabella the woman. The last five years hadn't happened yet…at least, not in her mind.

He looked down at her, his chest tight with wildly contradictory emotions. This was going to be so difficult. He didn't know how to deal with her…interact with her. He'd come to think of her as remote, sophisticated, self-contained but right now she was as bubbly and effervescent as a bottle of sparkling wine.

Again he told himself not to look ahead, not to think too much. All he could do was take life with Anabella one step at a time. He had to deal with one crisis before facing the next. And right now the girl wanted clean jeans.

In the bottom drawer of the dresser in her room he found old clothes that Anabella didn't wear anymore, but clothes she hadn't discarded, either.

Ana beamed. "Thank you." She grabbed a pair of jeans and an old cropped sweatshirt once a bright cherry red but through repeated washings had faded to brick. "I'll be ready in just a second. Should I meet you downstairs?"

He agreed and when she appeared fifteen minutes later she was dressed, her hair blow-dried, eye lashes thickened with mascara and lips darkened with a soft rosy lip gloss. "Better?" she teased.

"Much," Lucio nodded.

He wanted to smile at her but he couldn't. He was feeling so much, remembering so much. She exuded sweetness and spice, innocence and bravado. This was the Anabella he'd fallen in love with. This was the one he couldn't imagine living without.

But feeling this much was dangerous. He couldn't let his

emotions get the upper hand and he clamped down hard on all the chaotic, turbulent feelings rushing through him. What Anabella needed now was practical, rational support. She needed him calm. She needed him to remain firmly in control.

"We'll be eating in here," he said, steering her into the library. "I thought we could eat by the fire. It seemed cozy."

She blushed. "And intimate."

Intimate. Right. Not exactly the mood he was going for. But he let Anna's comment slide, focused instead on putting her at ease. It'd been a month since she sat at a real table for a meal, and Lucio hoped that this dinner together would be a first step for her on the road to recovery.

Neither said much during dinner but Ana ate nearly everything on her plate. It was a simple, traditional Argentine meal—grilled beef, *pommes frites,* green salad. "Thank God," she said, curling up in her wing chair, legs under her. "Real food again."

He was curious about her memory, about the past month and exactly what and how much she recalled. "What were you eating before?"

Ana shrugged. Smiled. Her teeth flashed white. "Isn't that odd? I don't remember. So it must not have been anything good, or I'd know, right?"

"That's one way of looking at it."

She laughed. "And what's another?"

His gut tightened and he watched the light from the fire dance and flicker across her expressive face. He loved her laugh, loved her when she was feisty and playful. When she teased him like this, he wanted to pull her onto his lap, into his arms, and keep her there forever.

Suddenly her expression grew somber and she dropped the French fry she'd been nibbling. "Lucio—"

"Yes, *negrita?*"

She blushed at the endearment. She'd always loved being his. "We're still going to get married, aren't we?" Her blush deepened. She seemed to be struggling with the words. "You do still want to marry me, don't you?"

So much innocence. Such a return to girlish dreams. For a moment he didn't know how to answer her. And then he thought, answer her honestly. Be truthful. She deserved that much. "Of course I want to marry you."

Her lips curved and her green eyes shone warm, soft, as though she were glowing from the inside out. "Really?"

"Yes."

"Then let's do it soon. I want to do it soon." She leaned forward. "How about tomorrow?"

CHAPTER FOUR

UPSTAIRS after dinner Anabella didn't want Lucio to leave her. She slid her arms around his waist, pressed close to him. "Stay with me," she whispered, her voice deepening, husky, voice of a seductress.

"I can't." He moved to kiss the top of her forehead before remembering that he wasn't her grandmother and he smiled to himself.

"Why not?"

And gazing down into her face, he realized all over again that all he could do was be as honest as possible. "I'm tired. I've just returned from a long trip and I need to sleep."

"You can sleep in my room."

"I wouldn't get any sleep, and neither would you." He stroked her soft cheek with the pad of his thumb. "And you need your rest as much as I do."

"I don't." And then she yawned and grinned a little. "Okay, maybe I do. But you'll be here later? You're not going away, are you?"

"I'll be here. I'm going nowhere. I'm staying here with you."

Lucio's room wasn't immediately next to Anabella's but down the hall, towards the end of the carpeted corridor. There was a small staircase at the end of the hall across from his room. The narrow staircase had been designed for the staff, but in the months since Lucio vacated the master bedroom, he'd found it convenient for him as well.

The sound of crying woke him. The sound was muffled and yet heart-rending.

It was Anabella crying. He heard her all the way down the hall and it wasn't the piercing shriek of earlier, but low

47

hoarse sobs. She was crying hard, crying into a pillow and she sounded utterly grief stricken. But why was she grieving? Had the illness perhaps resurfaced old memories and she was feeling again the loss of her father…the death of her brother Tadeo?

He slept naked and so leaving his bed, he quickly pulled on boxer shorts before heading to her room.

"Lucio," she looked up as he entered the room and held out a hand entreating.

He moved to the bed, sat down next to her, drawing her against him. She felt cold and she was shaking. "Did you have a bad dream?"

"No." Her teeth chattered. "Oh, it's worse than that. It's not a dream."

"What then could make you so upset?"

She wrapped her fingers around his and her hot tears fell on his arm. "You know, Lucio, you know already!"

"But I don't know—"

"You do and you have to forgive me. You must. Please, Lucio, tell me you'll forgive me."

What was she thinking right now? What was going through her head? "Ana, hush, you're needlessly upsetting yourself. There's nothing to forgive." Yet as soon as he said the words, he flashed back to last summer. He remembered the reports compiled by the private investigator.

Ana and another man. Ana in a hotel lounge with another man. He'd thought she was having an affair. It wasn't an affair. At least, the investigator never came up with anything conclusive. But she'd met with her mystery man on several occasions and she was so secretive about the meetings. She never mentioned them to Lucio, never discussed that part of her life with him.

His gut burned. He didn't want to think of that. Didn't want to remember that.

Her fingers squeezed his. "I can't do this anymore, I can't pretend. Can't forget." Her voice had dropped, and she shivered yet again. "We must get our baby back."

So she'd been dreaming, or having a nightmare. Either way, she was back to the baby again.

"Ana, there isn't a baby, there's never been a baby—"

"I was pregnant!" she retorted fiercely, pushing him away, her body taut with anger. "I was pregnant. That was why we were running away together. We were going to protect the baby."

"Yes, and you miscarried." And when she'd miscarried five years ago she'd become infertile.

They'd visited every specialist possible since then. Undergone countless tests without success. But Anabella had never completely accepted the diagnosis and privately Lucio blamed the demise of his marriage on the two and a half years of fertility treatments.

At least the infertility issue had been the first blow.

Or perhaps it was the last blow.

Lucio took her by the shoulders, held her before him. He forced her to meet his gaze. "But just because you can't conceive anymore, doesn't mean you'll never be a mother. There's always adoption—"

"I don't want to adopt, not when I have a baby!"

She wasn't going to let go of this one, was she? She had it in that poor confused head of hers that there really was a baby.

He caressed her cheek, and she looked up at him with wide pain-filled eyes. The pain in her eyes made him hurt. He hated for her to feel such loss, such confusion. This was so unfair. His heart hurt for her...for them. Lucio thought he'd never stop missing what they once had. What they'd once been.

"You really do love me," she whispered, her gaze riveted to his face.

"Of course."

She smiled, slowly, a tentative smile that started at the edge of her full lips and little by little transformed her face into breathtakingly beautiful.

And there went the hurt in his heart again. Anabella Galván Cruz owned him heart, body, mind and soul.

Ana couldn't look away from Lucio's beautiful face. His long hair was loose—she loved it down like this—and his chest was bare. He looked like the gaucho of her dreams. So hard and strong and fearless. Lucio could do anything. He could have anyone and he wanted her…

She felt a bubble of warmth form inside her and it was impossible to contain the sparkly joy. Leaning forward she brushed a fleeting kiss across his lips. "I'm so glad you're back. So glad you're home."

She'd been so afraid he'd changed his mind, so afraid that his silence and distance meant that his feelings for her had changed, too. "I thought perhaps you'd fallen in love with someone else," she said shyly. "You were gone such a long, long time."

His dark eyes met hers. "I didn't want to be, Ana. I wanted to be with you. You have to believe that."

She gently stroked her fingers across the smooth muscled plane of his chest. "So where were you?"

He seemed to struggle to find the words. "Working."

"Where?"

"Here. There."

Abruptly she looked up into his face. "We never did go see your family, did we?"

"No."

"Why not?"

Again he took a while to answer and she felt his resistance…reluctance. "Do they not want to meet me?"

"No, Ana." He exhaled slowly. "Things happened. And my father hasn't been well."

She waited, watching his face, watching his eyes. "Is he still sick?"

"He passed away a couple months ago."

Oh. Ana felt a lump rise to her throat. She knew how much Lucio loved his father, how much he'd admired him, too. Lucio's father had been a famous gaucho, a great gaucho from the North, not far from the banks of the Iguazu River, and his father had been a legend among his people.

"I'm so sorry," she whispered. And then the weight on her heart lightened. That's where he'd been. That's why he'd gone, why he'd left her so long.

He'd been with his father, with his family. Finally. It all made sense.

She curled against him, pressed her cheek to his chest, just above his heart. "I'd still like to meet your mother. And your brothers. It would mean a lot to me, Lucio. I think it'd be good for us."

And eventually she fell asleep nestled against him, her lips so close to his heart.

Lucio settled her back under the covers and then grabbed a spare pillow and blanket from the linen closet and stretched out on the floor of her room. It took him forever to fall asleep again but once he did, he didn't wake until the morning sun streamed through the open window.

Opening his eyes Lucio discovered Ana propped on her side watching him.

She smiled at him. *"Hola."*

He sleepily raked his hair back from his face. *"Hola."*

Anabella's smile grew. "You look beautiful." She stretched out and propped her chin in her hands without taking her eyes off of him. "I could never get tired of looking at you."

"Ana—"

"It's true. You've got a—" she broke off and made a little smacking sound, like that of a big loud kiss, "—perfect face."

"Ana."

"It's your eyes. No, your voice. No, your lips." Her mouth curved and her eyebrows arched. "I love your lips. The best lips in the whole world."

He made a rough sound and turned onto his back, folding his arms behind his head. She was so bad and so good and she was making his body hard. This isn't how he was supposed to be reacting to her. "And what?" he drawled, telling his body to relax because there was no way in hell anything was going to happen. "You've kissed all the lips in the world?"

His sarcasm made her laugh. "You've always been such a jealous boyfriend."

"Have not."

"Have so. I'm astonished that you're not wearing a fur loincloth and carrying a man-beating club."

He smiled on the inside and turned to look at her. Her long hair hung straight from her shoulders. Her full lips were a ripe, kissable pink. No one should look so sexy first thing in the morning. "Well, I do have a club, but you weren't supposed to know that. It's for emergencies only."

Her laughter echoed softly and she slipped from bed, moving to the carpet to sit next to him. "Have you ever killed anyone?"

"Ana!"

"Well, you've got a temper."

"I don't kill people, Ana."

"But you've gotten into plenty of fights, sí?"

"None that hurt anyone." That wasn't completely true but she didn't need the gory details, did she?

"Do you fight with your fists—"

He reached up and caught her wrist in his hand and tugged her down, to the carpet next to him. "What is this? Why the interest in fighting? Is there something you want me to do? Someone you want me to go take care of?"

Anabella felt a shiver race down her spine and she didn't know if it was his hand wrapped around her wrist or the husky inflection in his voice but she knew without a doubt he'd do anything for her. Absolutely anything.

He'd walk to the ends of the earth.

He'd enter a den of lions to save her.

Would he do it for their baby?

Ana sat still, very still, and she felt a peculiar prickle

across the top of her head, and the prickle turned to tiny sharp shudders up and down her spine. What a strange thought. What a weird thought.

His thumb brushed her pulse. "Where are you now, Ana?"

His voice was pitched so low, so tender and she felt her eyes burn. She blinked and shook her head. Where was she? Why here, of course. She was right here, in her bedroom with Lucio. And then she cocked her head as if listening to a voice in her head, a voice that was speaking in a very soft voice, or speaking very far away.

What were they doing here—she and Lucio—and whose bedroom was this anyway?

She frowned, looked at the carpet, at the wall, at the window. "Where are we?"

"In the villa, in Mendoza."

But that didn't sound right. It didn't seem to fit with anything she knew. She frowned again, her face stiff, her muscles weary. She felt lost. Submerged. As if she were beneath deep water and close to drowning. "Lucio?"

"Yes, *negrita*."

"Why are you here…sleeping in this room with me?"

He reached up and brushed a long strand of hair from her cheek. "You were sick."

She frowned, trying to remember being sick but there was nothing to recall. She remembered…nothing, at least, nothing out of the ordinary.

He was still combing her long hair back from her face. "Do you remember the hospital?" he asked.

She couldn't help coughing. Hospital? When? "No."

"You were in the hospital quite a while."

"A week?"

"A month."

Oh. That was definitely considerable time. She rubbed her temple as if sensing an invisible pain. "Did I take my exams?"

He just looked at her, didn't answer the question and she realized that maybe he didn't understand.

"Did I matriculate?" she persisted. "You know, graduate. Did I pass my exams?"

"At your school?"

"Yes."

His black lashes lowered over his dark brown eyes. "Yes."

That was a relief. "Good." She felt a little better, a little lighter. It was strange having him here, but it was good, too. Everything was better when Lucio was near.

But it still didn't make sense. How was it that he was sleeping in her bedroom? Mama wouldn't stand for it. Dante would have called the police. Nervously she slipped her hand into his, linking her fingers with his. "How did you get here, into my room?"

"You were sick. I had to be with you."

She liked that. He sounded so serious, so concerned. "But how did you convince Mama? She's such a snob, so prejudiced against anybody not from our circle."

A tiny muscle jumped in his cheek. "I didn't ask your mother's permission. This isn't your mother's house."

"Oh." So it *was* Dante's. She'd thought it must be Dante's. He had so many houses, so much money, he lived like a king. "And Dante let you?"

"Yes." Lucio sounded almost strangled.

"Good." She leaned forward and kissed Lucio lightly on the mouth. "I will take a shower and then we'll have breakfast, yes?"

Lucio called Dante as Anabella showered. Dante was already at his office in Buenos Aires.

"I told you I'd phone when there was a change in your sister's condition." Lucio didn't like calling Dante but he'd made a commitment. "There's a change in her condition."

There was a faint hesitation on the line and Lucio realized Dante was afraid, afraid to hear more bad news.

"For better or worse?" Dante asked.

"Better." Best not to drag this out. Just say what needed to be said and hang up. "Ana is more coherent today. She seems a lot more like the old Anabella."

"And her memory?"

"That hasn't returned."

"Ah."

Neither said anything for a moment and for the first time Lucio felt a kinship with Ana's brother. Ana needed her memories back. Ana needed her mistakes, triumphs, she needed her personal history. The Galváns were a complicated bunch. They'd lost the youngest brother, both older sisters had moved from Argentina, and Ana's own mother was too busy drinking to spend ten minutes with her daughter.

Ana's family history wasn't pretty and it wasn't easy but these were the things that Ana needed to remember. She wouldn't be able to move forward with her life until she reclaimed the past.

"She has photo albums from when she was younger," Dante said wearily. "Could you—would you—"

"I'll go through them with her."

Dante drew a short breath. "Tadeo was her best friend."

"I know."

"If it's too much—"

"I won't push it, and you already know, I won't push her." Lucio felt a heavy emotion weight his heart. He and Dante had spent so many years despising each other. What a waste of time. What a waste of life. "I will not hurt her. I won't let anyone hurt her."

Lucio hung up the phone to discover Ana standing in the doorway, a robe over her slender figure and her hair twisted in a towel. She'd just stepped from the shower and the dewy moisture of her skin made him ache to touch her, to taste her, to make her his again.

"Who was that?" she asked, leaning against the door frame.

"Dante."

Ana's expression immediately darkened. "What did he want now?"

Lucio moved towards her and pulled the towel from her hair, watching as the long damp tresses spilled down. "He was just checking to see if you felt better."

She made a face. "Tell him to send a card next time."

He tweaked her nose. "You're terrible."

She grinned a little. "Yes, but you like that about me."

Her mischievous smile made his body tighten, his gut hard as a rock. It was the craziest response. Hunger, fire, craving. He hadn't wanted her like this in years. She was making him feel so much again. She was making him feel everything again. It was like being back in those first weeks of heady infatuation, weeks where he could have sworn he could get by without eating or drinking, working or sleeping. All he wanted was to be with Anabella, to strip her naked and keep her bare and warm in his bed.

"You're right," he answered gruffly. "I do." And it crossed his mind in a whisper-soft voice, there was a part of him that would do anything, absolutely anything, to keep her in love with him.

Later that morning after Dr. Dominguez had arrived and checked on his patient, he gave Lucio an encouraging report. "She's definitely improving," the doctor said. "Whatever you're doing, keep it up."

"What about her memory?" Lucio asked as he walked the doctor to the door.

"That will return as Senora's strength returns. Just give her information in little bits. Don't overwhelm her with too much at one time. She'll still tire easily and if she tries to do too much too quickly, she could face some setbacks."

"What kind of setback?"

"Nothing serious, but she might experience new lapses in memory, tears, some mood swings. But that's all normal considering what she's been through. She's a remarkable woman, Senor and I'm very pleased with her recovery."

The doctor hesitated at the door. "And the nurse? Do you want her to continue monitoring your wife during the day?"

"I don't think it's necessary now that I'm home—" Lucio broke off, swallowed. *Back,* he silently corrected. He wasn't home. He was just back.

"Then we'll say today is Patricia's last day." The doctor stretched out his hand to shake Lucio's. "Call me if you need anything. Otherwise, I'll see Senora at my office in ten days."

"Sounds good."

But the day didn't go smoothly. Anabella didn't understand why Patricia was staying even through the day. She didn't want to remain at the villa, either. In her room she tossed clothes into a small travel bag before she came tearing back down the stairs.

"Let's go," she cried, the heels of her stiletto black boots echoing against the terra-cotta tiles in the entry hall as she headed for the open front door. She wore a black T-shirt and body hugging jeans, her long black hair roped in a loose ponytail with inky wisps falling around her face.

Lucio heard her footsteps and turned on the front step. Everyone knew he had a weakness for horses and fast cars, and when Ana appeared in the doorway, dressed like a sexy Hollywood starlet, Lucio knew he had a weakness for fast women.

Anabella was unlike any other woman he'd ever known.

"Are we going?" she said, dropping her canvas and leather travel bag at his feet.

"Ana."

"*Sí,* Senor?" she mocked, hands on slim hips, head thrown back and the sun danced in her eyes, reflecting bright glints of emerald and jade.

Lucio scooped up Ana's travel bag and took her arm, leading her back into the house. "You're not strong enough to travel yet."

"Ridiculous!" She tugged her arm free as he shut the

front door behind them. "I feel great. I'm as fit as I've ever been."

"You are improving," he agreed. "But you're not one hundred per cent yet, and you've got to take it easy a little longer—"

Her cheeks flushed. "I'm not an old lady, Lucio!"

"I never said you were."

"But you're treating me like one! You're keeping me trapped here, a prisoner, just like Dante."

Lucio's patience snapped. "I'm not like Dante!" he retorted sharply. "And if I sound like Dante then maybe it's because you're acting like a spoiled kid."

Her mouth opened and shut and she stared at him wordlessly, her eyes filling with tears. And then shaking her head she dashed back up the stairs to her room, and her bedroom door slammed behind her.

Lucio stood at the foot of the stairs looking up, past the gently curving banister. *Damn.*

He couldn't do this. He didn't know how to do this. He and Anabella had never had a relationship like this before. They'd always been partners. Equals. But nothing felt equal anymore.

She resented the authority he wielded.

He resented being forced into an authoritarian role.

What he'd loved about Ana was her freedom, her spirit, her fire. With her he felt optimism, possibility, imagination.

But after several years of marriage all the imagination was gone, the mystery and possibility stripped bare, and he realized now they'd become just ordinary people with everyday lives.

The very thing neither he nor Anabella had ever wanted.

Anabella curled up in the down-filled cream and wine striped armchair in her room and cried as if her heart would break.

Lucio had changed.

He could say everything was fine, he could say his feelings hadn't changed, but he wasn't the same.

She felt the glass wall that had formed between them. She could see him, she could see his mouth moving, but she felt no warmth from him. It was as if he was just going through the motions. Saying scripted words but they weren't his words. They weren't words from his heart.

Ana drew a raw breath, her throat aching, and wiped tears from her face. Turning her head she rested her damp cheek on her bent knee and stared out at the snowcapped Andes visible through her bedroom window.

What exactly had happened, she wondered? Had he fallen out of love with her? Had his feelings changed? Become less sexual…more fraternal?

There was a firm knock on her door and her door opened. Lucio entered.

"Did I forget to take my medicine or something?" she flashed, barely glancing at him before turning her gaze back to the window.

"No. Although I'm sure I could find something evil tasting if you'd like."

She lifted her chin. "Are you making fun of me?"

"A little," he smiled.

Ana felt a wave of emotion rush through her. Hunger, longing, need. He'd been part of her world so long she couldn't imagine life without him. "Why are you mad at me?" she asked, turning to look at him.

"I'm not mad," he said, approaching. He carried several large leather books. "I'm short on sleep."

"So go sleep!"

His lips curved. "Can't. I've got you to entertain." He leaned over and lifted her with one arm, and she felt the hard muscle in his arm, the warmth of his skin, the spicy scent of him envelop her. "Come, *chica,* be a good girl and sit with me. We're going to look at something."

She wanted to be mad at him, wanted to give him a good elbow in his ribs but she loved the caressing note in his voice as he called her little girl and the ease with which he held her.

Dante and her mother had always wanted to contain her, curtail her, put limits on her. Lucio had always set her free.

She wanted to be free.

Lucio knew she loved to be free.

Glancing up, she glimpsed Lucio's square jaw and firm flat chin and the shadow of his beard. He hadn't shaved yet this morning. She was glad. She loved it when he didn't shave, loved his long hair and his broad shoulders, loved the taut muscles cording his thighs.

Ana reached up and lightly stroked his jaw with the short black bristles. The rasp of his beard was such a contrast to the softness of his mouth. He was like that. Hard on the outside. Gentle on the inside.

He wouldn't be here if he didn't love her.

Impulsively she pressed a light kiss to the corner of his mouth, catching both beard and his amazing lips. ''So show me the pictures, *carnino*. I am all yours.''

CHAPTER FIVE

"DO YOU know who this is?" Lucio asked, drawing his arm around Ana as he pointed to a photograph of an unsmiling teenage girl standing next to a much younger version of Dante. The pictures in the first photo album they leafed through had already begun to age.

The album was full of photos of babies and young children, of an imperious stone estate surrounded by tall iron gates, of a smiling Mama and Papa with cocktail glasses raised as if toasting yet another beautiful day in Buenos Aires.

They'd leafed through all silently but it was the photo of the unsmiling teenage girl that had caught Lucio's attention. The girl in the photo was wearing a school uniform, white blouse, dark pleated skirt, ankle socks and dark shoes, and yet despite the girlish uniform she managed to look elegant, refined. You could see the intelligence in her fine, aristocratic features, you could see the pain, too. There was no hope in her somber dark eyes.

"Paloma." Ana reached out, touched the picture gently, almost caressing the pale face with the pinched mouth and sad eyes. "Dante's sister. My half sister."

"What happened to her?"

They'd never discussed Paloma before. There'd never been a need to discuss Paloma. "She ran away. To America." Ana chewed on her lip. "I don't remember her very well. I was seven when she left and I've never seen her again."

Lucio bent his head, studied her half sister's photograph. "She looks so unhappy."

"Papa and her mama arranged a marriage for her. Paloma

refused. Her mama locked her in her room for weeks to punish her. Tadeo was the one who unlocked her door. Paloma left that night and Papa disowned her. Said she was as good as dead.''

They flipped through another few pages, stopping at a series of pictures taken on the beach. "Mar del Plata?" Lucio guessed, naming one of Argentina's most popular, and elegant beach resorts.

"We had a house there. We went every summer, just after the first of the new year." Ana smiled at the picture of her, Estrella and Tadeo on the beach posing in their new swimsuits. She remembered that trip, remembered how grown up they thought they were. They'd become teenagers, Estrella nearly seventeen, Ana just turned thirteen, Tadeo in the middle.

Every guy they met that summer fell for Estrella. They chased after her, followed her around, showed up at their beach house in droves. And Estrella had been oblivious.

Estrella with her beautiful face and beautiful body didn't want a boyfriend. She wanted to become a missionary and save the world.

"Guys were crazy about Estrella," she said, intentionally avoiding talking—or thinking—about Tadeo. Far easier to think about her sisters. Tadeo's death was something she'd never come to grips with.

"She's almost as beautiful as you," Lucio said, kissing the top of her head.

"More beautiful. She became a model in Italy after Father wouldn't let her join the Peace Corps. His daughter could wear fancy clothes but she couldn't get dirty." Ana tried to smile but her heart had begun to ache, bittersweet emotion washing through her, one after the other.

"So you and Dante are the only ones still in Argentina," Lucio concluded quietly, summing up the very thing Ana had been thinking.

Ana's eyes burned and she swallowed hard. It was true. One way or another, she'd lost them all.

Except for Dante.

Except for the big brother who'd stayed and shouldered the family business, the family heartaches, the family name.

"I don't hate him," she whispered, blinking at the tears scalding her eyes. "I love Dante."

Lucio wrapped his hand around her ponytail. "I know you do."

She shut the album and lifted it to her chest, holding it tightly against her, holding it to her heart. "All he's ever wanted is the best for me." Lucio didn't speak and she squeezed her eyes shut. It was so hard, so much harder than she ever let anyone know.

As much as she adored Dante, she still missed Tadeo terribly. There wasn't a day she didn't think of him. Tadeo had been the sane one, the gentle one, the one with a heart as big as the plains. He never judged. He never criticized. He had been her rock and her constant and her friend. And when he'd died she wished she'd died, too.

"Dante was living in New York when Tadeo overdosed," she said, reaching up to brush a stray tear away. "Dante had a girlfriend and a job in New York and he loved the city. But when Tadeo died, Dante gave up everything in New York and came home and he's been the way you know him ever since."

"He tries to protect you." Lucio's voice was tender.

"Because he doesn't want to be the only one." Ana felt the grief inside her, huge, hot, overwhelming. "And I can't blame him. I don't want to be the only one, either."

Lucio wrapped his arm around her and drew her close to his chest. She was crying hard, her shoulders shook, and yet he thought that perhaps this is just what she needed. In all their years together she'd never talked much about her family. She'd never mentioned Paloma, or why Estrella had gone to Italy. Ana had brought up Tadeo several times and yet she couldn't say much more than his name.

Today, for the first time, she'd given him a real glimpse of her family. Not the glossy photos of the Galváns published in the different society and entertainment magazines, but the family Ana knew, the family Ana had been part of.

Once her family had been closer, more tight-knit, but the family of her childhood had given way, eroded by time and anger and death.

No wonder Anabella had been so quick to run away with him five years ago. She was running from the shell of what had been, desperate for something new.

As he gently rocked her in his arms, Lucio felt the second photo album bump his hip. The second album was the album Anabella had put together of them, and he'd hoped to go through that album this afternoon, to study the pictures of two of them together, but with Ana's hot tears splashing on his neck he knew she couldn't handle too much more right now.

She was still emotionally fragile. She was still recovering from a terrible illness. He'd started laying the groundwork for piecing together her memory, but he'd done as much as he could right now. Obviously she wasn't ready for him to pour out the facts of his and her troubled relationship.

First, she needed time to grieve. She needed to mourn the changes in her family, the death of Tadeo, and most of all, she needed to cry for herself, as Ana hadn't just lost members of her family. She'd lost huge pieces of her heart.

A little later, with her face still buried against Lucio's chest, Ana realized she had to stop crying. Lucio's shirt was soaked and she was getting stiff. Lifting her head she looked up at Lucio and he said nothing but he looked worried.

And the last thing she needed was Lucio getting himself all worked up over her again.

"I'm okay," she said, sniffling and plucking at his wet shirt. "But you might want to change."

"Mmmm." He kissed her forehead and then laughed as he must have caught sight of her irritated expression. "Oops, forgot."

"Sure you did." She unwound herself and climbed off his lap. "If you'll just excuse me."

Ana disappeared into the bathroom, washed her face, combed her hair and applied a little makeup to cover her pink nose and puffy eyes.

She emerged from the bathroom considerably more composed. "An improvement, yes?" she said, indicating her gleaming brushed hair and freshly made up face.

"I don't know. I kind of like the hysterical virgin." He rose, stretching to his full height.

"Virgin?" It always amazed Ana, how tall he was, how well built. He had such broad shoulders and impossibly long legs. "I haven't been a virgin since you took care of that a while ago." She'd never forget that night, their first night together. She hadn't told him she was a virgin. He had no idea she was only seventeen, in her last year at school, or the aristocratic daughter of a count. She'd told him nothing. He'd asked no questions. And it'd been the most wonderful night of her life.

"Well, you'll always be my virgin," he answered, and his smile was so warm, so intimate she was certain he remembered that first night, too.

"You collect virgins, then?"

"No. I just want you."

His gaze held hers so long she grew warm, her body heating, tingling. She felt the intensity in his dark eyes like a caress on her cheek, a touch to her breast. He might as well have taken her in his arms and put his hands on her burning skin.

He knew how she felt, too. She was certain he knew her body felt liquid and hot and crazy with need.

When had they last made love? When had they been naked and alone and free with each other?

"Has it been a long time since we—" she broke off, touched her tongue to her upper lip, wondering at the dryness of her mouth, at the pounding of her heart. "Since we…had sex?"

Sex. Why had she said sex? Why hadn't she called it love? They never had sex. They'd always *made love.*

Ana saw the way his eyes narrowed and heat prickled across her face. She felt so naked all of sudden. So exposed in ways that had nothing to do with her question, or their conversation.

Something was different between them. He was different. Or was it her?

"It's been a while," he answered evenly, calmly.

Yet he wasn't calm on the inside. She knew because she saw the fire in his eyes. She saw the flicker of emotion, and his deep feelings were like flames dancing. What he felt was both new and familiar.

He'd missed her.

He wasn't really hers.

He wanted to be hers.

What did it all mean?

Ana closed her eyes, thinking that if there was something bad, she didn't want to know, wasn't ready to know.

If he'd found a new love…if he'd made a new life for himself…she'd really rather wait before he told her. She'd rather have one perfect day with him—and one perfect night—before the bad news came.

"You look like Paloma and Estrella." Lucio's husky voice broke the quiet. "So sad. But don't be sad, *flaca*. You don't ever have to be sad when I'm here."

He'd called her buddy, friend; it was such a casual endearment and yet so perfect for everything they'd ever been together. Buddy, pal, friend, lover.

She moved to him, placed her hands on his flat stomach and slowly slid her palms up, across his chest, feeling the smooth curve of muscle, the strong hard plane. "Then promise me you'll always stay."

He caught her face in his hands and stared at her as if she were something so precious and yet so fleeting. As if she were a dream. A cloud. A mirage. "I will stay until you ask me to leave."

"Never," she whispered.

His jaw worked and he swallowed. His dark eyes took on a sheen. "Never is an awfully long time."

"Yes," she said, lifting her hands to wrap them around his wrists, keeping his hands pressed to her face. "And you said the same thing about forever. But I'm not afraid of time, and I'm not afraid of life, and the only thing I fear is us not being together. That would truly be forever. That, Lucio, would be eternity."

Lucio couldn't breathe. He dragged in a raw breath but it didn't help. Nothing helped.

He had to leave here. He couldn't do this. He had to tell her the truth.

She was his wife. She'd hated their marriage. She'd been the one to divorce him.

Tell her. Tell her, you fool, tell her before she breaks your heart all over again. Tell her what you must tell her and get this miserable pain over with.

But she was looking up at him with such love, her green eyes warm, her lovely face so alive, and in her warm eyes he saw the hope and faith he'd carried alone for the past year.

It was as if she'd picked up the mantle, assumed the warrior role. She believed in them.

She believed in the two of them standing together, shoulder to shoulder, confronting the world.

His head dipped, his mouth covered hers. He couldn't do this, shouldn't do this, but he had to have just this one kiss. He had to feel her and touch her, smell her and taste her and save this kiss for forever's sake.

I love you. The words were there in his head as his mouth brushed hers, parting hers, drawing her breath into him. *I love you, mi amor. I love everything you are, and everything we were.*

The bedroom door suddenly opened and Lucio guiltily lifted his head. Patricia the nurse stood in the doorway, a tray in her arms. "Lunch for Senora," she said.

"You can put it on the table." Lucio stepped back from

Anabella. He felt sick inside. He felt despicable. He couldn't do this to Ana, couldn't take advantage of her.

"Would you like me to bring you up a tray, Senor?" the nurse asked, arranging Ana's lunch on the table.

"No. Thank you."

"But Senor, you haven't eaten anything today. Let me get you a tray."

"I'm fine," he answered brusquely, increasingly disgusted. He'd come here with the photo albums to help jog Ana's memory and instead he'd only tangled them both in knots.

But the nurse's brow creased with concern. "I know you're not sleeping, Senor. You must be tired. You should at least try to rest a little."

"Thank you." He nodded to both of them, and without another word, left the room.

What was he doing here? What was he doing to Anabella? If he cared about her, if he truly loved her, he'd tell her the truth. He'd give her the facts she needed instead of taking part in this distortion of reality.

Lucio spent the rest of the afternoon shut up in his old study, working on his laptop, answering e-mails, returning phone calls. He found that if he worked hard enough, and concentrated intently, he could forget everything but the winery business before him.

Lucio was still hunched over his desk late in the afternoon when his office door creaked open. "The big bad wolf has gone," Ana said in a mock stage whisper. "We're safe. We're free to play."

Lucio bit the inside of his cheek as he leaned back in his chair. Ana hadn't just referred to Nurse Patricia as the big bad wolf, had she? "Who are you talking about?"

Ana grimaced. "That busybody. The one that likes you more than she likes me."

He had to work very hard to keep his expression blank. "I don't think that's the case," he said, pleased to see Ana despite everything. There was no one in the world he liked better. No one he loved more.

"Oh no? Then who am I? *Oh Senor, you poor thing! Are you tired? You must be tired!*" Ana put her hands on her hips. "Senor, does that sound about right?"

The impression he thought, pushing away from his desk, was a little too good. "Not sure who you're trying to imitate."

"*But you look so hungry. Let me feed you. You are starving, Senor. You are weak. Let me unbutton my dress. I have something very special to give you—*"

He pressed a finger to her lips, silencing her, not knowing if he should be amused or chagrined. "You're jealous!" he told her.

The tip of her tongue flicked across his palm and his body tightened as she licked him again, her tongue wet and cool against his warm skin. It felt too good. He loved her mouth on him, but he couldn't let her do this.

And then he let out a yell as she bit him. "What the devil?" he swore and pulled his hand from her teeth.

"Am not jealous," Ana said sweetly. "Just telling you what I've seen."

He examined the sharp teeth marks on his hand. "You're an animal."

"I know." She grinned, wrapped her arms around his waist and rubbed herself against him. "Now take me for a walk."

"Like a puppy dog?"

She nearly bit him again. "No, like a panther on a leash."

Ana sighed with pleasure as they left the house and stepped outside, onto the covered patio with the tall stately columns.

A cool breeze ruffled her hair and she lifted her face to the sky. "I miss being outside," she said. "I wish we'd do this more."

In the distance the sun glowed behind the mountains and

the sky looked purple with a top layer of pink and red. "It's going to be a beautiful night," he agreed.

The villa was situated high enough on the hill to give them views of the valley and town and the lights beginning to sparkle in bits of yellow and white.

As she studied the horizon, Ana felt a peculiar ache. "Everything feels so dreamy. Kind of surreal." She glanced at Lucio. "Does it ever feel that way to you?"

A small muscle pulled in his jaw. "All the time."

"Maybe it's being here, in this house, but I feel like Alice in Wonderland. Time seems mixed up. Life seems mixed up. I almost feel like I can see the past and the future at the same time."

He shot her a swift side glance. "And what do you see?"

She moved closer to him, sliding an arm around his waist and burying her fingers in the back pocket of his trousers. Her heart was beating faster, harder. "I see—I see—" she drew another quick breath but she couldn't continue.

She was afraid to say what she thought. It wasn't as if she knew details, facts. It was just a sense of foreboding. Like seeing dark clouds gathering on the horizon.

"I see a walk," she said instead, dropping her arm from his waist, suddenly grateful she'd worn a sweater over her black T-shirt. She felt cold on the inside. Icy. There were things Lucio hadn't told her and she didn't even know how to uncover the unknown.

Take it slowly, she told herself, sliding her hands up inside the sleeves of her sweater. *No reason to rush it. It's been a good day. But then, every day with Lucio is a good day. And he's here. That's what you want, isn't it?*

"You'll be warm enough?" Lucio asked, glancing down at her.

He must have seen her shiver. She forced a smile and nodded. It was hard to hide her fear. "Yes. I've my sweater. Thanks."

They descended the patio's steps into the garden, heading down the boxwood bordered path.

Gravel crunched beneath their feet and the first of the antique roses were blooming, scenting the air, and Anabella would have said it was romantic if Lucio's mood wasn't so gloomy.

"Did something happen between us?" she asked after a moment as they passed the herb garden with the little sundial. "Did we have a fight? Something to do with the baby?"

"No."

She saw his jaw harden, felt him withdraw. Something had happened, though. "Was I mad at you because you weren't there with me when I lost the baby?"

His eyes narrowed. "Were you angry that I wasn't with you?"

"I was angry that I didn't get to keep the baby."

"The baby was born prematurely. The baby didn't survive."

She shook her head. "I don't believe that. I think there's a baby. I really do."

They'd stopped walking. He stared down at her. "How old are you?" he asked abruptly.

She felt a wave of outrage. How rude. How *arrogant.* Here she was, talking about their missing child, and he wanted to know how old she was? "Are you trying to be funny?"

"No."

"What kind of question is that? Is it a trick question?"

"No, Ana." His voice was hard. His face was hard. Suddenly everything about him was stony. "Answer the question."

"I'm eighteen, and that's the silliest question."

He muttered something she didn't understand and he walked away from her, long angry strides carrying him back to the house. She ran to catch up with him.

"What's wrong with you?" she demanded, stopping him on the arbor-covered patio. Lights glowed in scattered candles. Strings of white lights were woven through the branches of patio trees. "And don't give me any more of your patronizing bullshit! I know something's wrong. Tell me what it is."

Lucio shook his head, his dark brows pulled, his features tight. He didn't say anything. He just kept shaking his head.

"Is this about me? Did I do something wrong?"

"No, Anabella. Just leave it alone."

"I can't! Not when I know there's a problem—"

"Yes, there was a problem. You were sick. I was worried. They said you might die. It's been hard, Anabella."

"But I didn't die. I'm here and I want to be with you."

"It takes time—"

"*What* does?"

"Adjusting. Getting used to this." His voice was harsh and his words were delivered in short, sharp bursts. "I'm glad you're better, but part of me doesn't know what to do."

"There's nothing to do. I'm getting better every day."

He nodded once, his dark hair pulled sleekly back from his face emphasizing the high cheekbone, the angle of his jaw, the square chin.

She reached out to touch his face, to trace the beautiful line of cheekbone. He flinched at the brush of her fingers. "I'm getting better," she insisted.

He nodded again but he wouldn't look at her and she felt a stab of fear. Just like the dark foreboding feelings of earlier, she again had the peculiar sensation of seeing the past and the future at the same time.

"Maybe you're still worried," she said, wanting him to say something and when he didn't, feeling compelled to fill the silence.

"I know what death is, Lucio. Death is permanent. Illness is not." She ducked her head and worked on buttoning her thin burnt orange cardigan.

"I was the one that found Tadeo." She forced the words out, forced herself to keep speaking. "I never told you. But I was the one who discovered Tadeo in his bed. I was the one to call for help. I was the one who stayed with him until the ambulance came because mother had passed out—and Father…'' her voice faded as she went back, remembering back.

Paloma going. Estrella going. Her father's spectacular car crash two years after Estrella moved to Italy. He'd left their estancia in San Antonio de Areco late one Sunday night for the city, made a fatal miscalculation on the narrow single-lane highway, and that was the end of that. The end of Count Tino Galván.

Then Tadeo. *Tadeo*.

''Burying Tadeo could have been the end of me.'' She was surprised at the firmness of her voice, the steely note beneath the ache. ''But then I met you. You changed everything. You took the broken pieces of my heart and you made it new again. You gave me hope.''

She lifted her head, looked at him. ''You still do.''

He groaned softly, turned his head away.

''Why do you do that?'' she demanded hotly, eyes burning. ''Why can't you look at me? Why are you so afraid to touch me? You treat me now as if I'm something dangerous. *Toxic*.''

''You're not toxic.'' His voice was rough. ''You're far from toxic.''

''But?''

''There's no but. You're beautiful. You're smart. You're sexy. Funny—'' He broke off, looked up at the sky. ''I didn't have a painful childhood. I grew up happy. I felt lucky. Blessed.''

He turned to look at her. ''And then I got you.''

''And it was the beginning of the end, right?''

The bitterness in her voice made him flinch. ''No, Ana, it was the beginning of the beginning. I realize I'd never lived until I met you. I realized I'd only lived for me. You changed me. You opened the world to me.''

His expression was hard and yet his voice was soft. ''You taught me the meaning of love. You taught me the meaning of life. I changed forever." His lips curved in a ghost of a smile. "All because of you."

"How?"

"Oh, Ana, you should know this part. You, Anabella Galván, made love real to me. I had a mother, and I had a father, but their love was nothing compared to the love I felt from you. The love I felt *for* you." He fell silent a moment, considering her. "Because of you, I'm a different person today."

Her heart ached. "Is that good or bad?"

"It was good."

"Sounds wonderful," she whispered.

"It was."

Why couldn't she take this all in? Why didn't it feel right? There was something missing... "Yet you speak only in the past tense. Did we lose it, Lucio?"

"No. Yes." His shoulders rose and fell. "We both said and did things. We made mistakes."

"So we did have a fight."

"It wasn't a fight. It...we..." his shoulders lifted, shrugged, a helpless gesture from the least helpless man she'd ever met. "Oh, Ana, I suppose we just grew up."

CHAPTER SIX

ANA was afraid to learn more, and yet she couldn't stop now. She had to keep asking the questions that would let her put all the pieces of her past together.

Like what happened between them. And the fate of their baby.

Nervous, she drew a deep breath. "What about the baby?" she whispered, fingers threading, kneading. "Did we ever find him?"

"Ana."

She ground her teeth together, fighting for calm. "You don't want me to talk about it, and you don't like to hear about it, but there is a baby, Lucio. We *did* have a baby."

Lucio felt a wave of tenderness, and sadness. Poor Anabella. She'd never accepted the loss of their child, nor accepted that she'd never be able to bear another child.

She'd miscarried fairly far along in her pregnancy and in an effort to stem the hemorrhaging, she'd been hurt, her insides scarred to the point that she could no longer conceive again. Although God knows they tried. And tried. And Anabella had put herself through hell trying to get her body "fixed."

"Ana, you've talked a great deal about a baby," he said quietly. "But there isn't a baby. You lost the baby."

"I didn't."

"You did." He took her arm, felt her resistance, but ignored it, just as he ignored the hard set of her jaw.

"We do have a child," she said bitterly. "We do. It's a boy, too."

Lucio battled to hang on to his patience. The doctor had predicted that Anabella would continue to have memory issues, as well as some mood changes. He tried to view this as just a small setback. Nothing serious. And slowly he walked her along the veranda, the moon beginning to rise and the little lights in the potted trees glowing like fireflies.

"Lucio, are you listening to me?"

"Yes." He had to continue to support her. He needed to listen to her, try his best to be objective with her. And yet could she have picked a more painful, difficult subject to obsess over?

"So where is this child, Ana?" he asked calmly. "Where does he live? Who is taking care of him?"

She shuddered a little. "I don't know. And that's why we must find him, Lucio, we must bring him home."

He sat down on one of the lounge chairs on the end of the veranda and drew her down next to him. She sat close to him, her hip and shoulder brushing his.

It was bittersweet sitting here like this. Sitting this close it reminded him of the way their skin felt when they were naked. Reminded him of her hands on his hips and his body pressed against hers.

But he couldn't think about making love, couldn't think about the things he missed. He had to help Ana, had to understand what was happening in her head.

"*Negrita,* if there really was a baby, if we'd had a son, you would have told me," he said kindly. "I know you, Anabella. You couldn't keep this sort of thing hidden from me. You wouldn't be able to hide it."

Her dark green eyes filled with tears and she looked away, her small firm profile set but her lower lip quivered. "But what if I did?" she whispered. "What if I did keep it a secret and what if the pain of it ate and ate at me until I couldn't sleep, eat, think straight?"

He looked at her unable to think of a single thing to say. Either she was terribly confused, or she'd hidden a huge part of her inner life from him.

She knotted her hands. "I'd hoped to find the baby before

you returned. I've been trying to find the baby but I've lost track of him, lost all my leads.''

He covered her hands with one of his. "I think you expect too much of yourself right now—"

"I'm not crazy!"

He tensed inwardly. "I never said you were."

"No, but you're implying it. And I'm telling you," she caught at his hand, her fingers gripping his tightly. "I'm telling you the truth. We have a baby. He did not die. He was supposed to be given back to me as soon as I recovered from the delivery, but they did not give him back. They took him and they—" she drew a deep breath, "—sold him.''

Lucio felt his stomach heave and he stood. Anabella's nonsense was getting to him. Her disturbed imagination was out of control and as much as he wanted to help her, he didn't think he could. Not if she talked like this. Not if she said such horrible, hateful things.

A baby. A son. Kept from his mother and then sold.

Sold.

Maybe Anabella had lost her mind.

Lucio tugged at the collar of his shirt, found it far too tight and began to work at the buttons, loosening the fabric so he could feel air on his skin, loosening the choke hold so he could breathe.

Not even aware that he'd left her, just knowing he needed space, Lucio walked back into the house, down the wide cool hall towards the front door. He'd get his car. He'd go for a drive. He'd try to calm down.

"Lucio!"

Her voice pierced the cool quiet hall lit with small antique sconces. He didn't want to stop. He wanted to ignore her frightened cry but he couldn't.

He hesitated even though in his heart, part of him was still leaving.

"It's true, Lucio.'' Her voice floated down the hall, soft, tentative and yet the words were clear enough in his head.

"And I need you to help me. I need you to help me locate the baby. *Please.*"

He turned slowly, turning his back on the front door. He was so close to freedom. So close to escaping, and he did need to escape. Even if just for a little bit.

If he were honest, he'd admit that this aspect of Anabella's illness overwhelmed him. He could handle broken bones, scars and wounds, but this…this confusion in her head…it was as if Ana wasn't even Ana anymore.

"I'm just going to go out for a little while," he said. "I'll be back for a late dinner. I'm just going to go back to my office, tidy up some things—"

"I have proof."

Her voice quavered indignantly. He stared down the hall at her, unable to think of a single thing to say.

"I do."

She led him upstairs, to her bedroom and then stopped, stared around. "Where is it?"

"Where is what?" Lucio asked wearily.

"My things. The baby's things."

"I've never seen anything for a baby among your things."

Ana touched a hand to her temple. Her head was thumping, hard. Nothing was making sense. She knew she had all the papers, all her information, in a box. It was a blue box. Light blue, almost like the sky, and it had very thin white stripes. "I know. I've always kept it hidden. But it's just a shoe box, a blue shoe box. Maybe Maria put it somewhere."

"I haven't seen a blue shoe box."

She felt tears start to her eyes. "Well, you don't know everything!"

"And neither do you!"

They were both breathing hard and they glared at each other from across her room. She hated him at that moment. She really did. He was so arrogant, so sure he was right. But what did he know? What had he bothered to find out?

"So what don't I know?" she demanded.

"Time's passed."

"I know."

"A lot of time has passed."

Her heart had begun to pound. Furiously, she pressed her nails into her palms. "How much?"

"Five years."

Ana wobbled and with a soft exhale, her legs nearly went out from beneath her. If Lucio hadn't moved forward quickly, she would have fallen. Instead he caught her, steadied her.

Despite her protests, he swung her into his arms and carried her to her bed and immediately reached for his phone.

"You're not calling the doctor." Her voice echoed with disbelief. "There's no reason to call the doctor. I wobbled—"

But Lucio ignored her. "Yes, Stephen, she collapsed right in front of me—"

"I didn't collapse! That wasn't a collapse!" Ana shouted, trying to drown out Lucio. "I wobbled. Lost my balance. I didn't faint."

Lucio glowered at her, his black brows flattening.

"Oh, knock it off," she flashed, trying to grab the phone from him. "You're not in charge around here!"

"The hell I'm not!" Lucio retorted grimly before turning his attention back to the doctor. "Yes, she recovered immediately. No, she didn't lose consciousness."

"I'm fine," Ana insisted.

Lucio pointed at the pillows. "Lie down."

Who was he kidding? She almost laughed out loud and made another swipe for his phone. "I'm not sick. I was shocked. I still am. Now give me the phone!"

With a mighty lunge she managed to wrench the phone from Lucio's hand. "*Hola*, Stephen, *sí*, everything's fine. I merely lost my balance. I never lost consciousness. This is nothing serious. Tell my husband—" she broke off horrified, and looked up at Lucio. She felt her heart pound, fast and furious. Ana licked her dry lips. "Tell my...husband...I am fine."

Numbly she handed the phone back to Lucio before sitting back down in the middle of the bed.

She was married to Lucio.

How did she know that? How did she remember?

Married to Lucio. When? How? Where? Impossible. But he'd said five years had gone by...

Was it possible?

She heard rather than saw Lucio say his goodbyes to the doctor and hang up the phone. He clipped the phone onto his belt. For a long moment her room was dark and still.

"You remembered." Lucio broke the silence.

She sat frozen in place, her thoughts like leaves blown by the autumn wind. She couldn't quite contain the direction of her thoughts, or their spin. "If it's been five years..." her voice drifted away and she bit her lower lip.

Five missing years. Five years where she remembered nothing other than Lucio was her husband.

"You're almost twenty-three," he continued quietly.

Ana was grateful for the dusky shadows in her room. She felt incredibly foolish. Vulnerable.

Lucio moved to the table next to her bed and turned on the brass lamp with the gold and black shade.

Ana averted her head from the lamp's gold glow. She didn't want to see anything, didn't want to discuss anything now. "Can this wait a little bit? I need some time."

"We have to talk."

"No." Her fingers balled against her knees. "Not now."

"You wanted to talk earlier. You insisted we talk downstairs—"

"But that was before!" she cried, voice breaking. "That was when I thought...when I thought..."

"When you thought what, *mi mujer?*" he asked gently.

My wife. My woman.

Ana's eyes burned but there weren't any tears left. She

felt hot and cold, nervous. She was married to Lucio. She'd been married for years.... It was all so overwhelming.

Lucio felt her tense as he circled the bed. Her hands shook as she pressed her palms against her knees. He saw the faint tremor in her fingers. The swanlike arch of her neck.

Funny how the earth could move and the heavens could open and everything change—everything but his intensely physical awareness of her.

From the first time he'd seen her, he'd felt her. Felt her like a wall of heat, a shaft of ice, a rock thrown at the back of his head.

And she had thrown a rock, early on, in one of their first fights. He learned the hard way, that she had a great arm and perfect aim. The rock hit him hard on the back of his head and drew blood.

Negrita. Such a spitfire. She'd always been hell on wheels and it'd been everything he'd ever wanted.

"Don't smile," she said, kneeling stiffly.

"Why not? You make me smile." He suddenly felt savage, his anger burning him alive. How could this have happened? How could this tragedy happen on top of all the others?

They were meant to be together. They were supposed to stay together. Why had she divorced him? Why had she wanted to leave him?

He clenched his back teeth, sucked in his stomach, muscles knotted from top to bottom. "At least, you used to make me smile."

Her dark head tipped and she slowly looked up at him. His gut tightened as her eyes briefly met his, the green like the priceless emeralds mined in Colombia.

"You loved to provoke me," he continued, "just as you loved to provoke everyone. You were so headstrong. You gave your family fits, especially your brother. Dante was always so worried about you."

She sat quiet for so long he thought perhaps she'd floated

away, her mind escaping into another place as it had just after the accident when she couldn't focus for more than a few minutes at a time.

"I don't remember," she said at last.

"I know."

She bent her head, hiding her face again, and her long black hair gleamed down her back like an ebony waterfall. "I might not ever remember."

His stomach felt like it was on fire. He practically devoured antacids, the worry chewing his stomach up, making it burn night and day. "Then we start over."

She looked up again, her intense green gaze full of dread and cynicism. "Over?"

"Yes." He forced himself to smile, forced calm when he felt like picking up the chair in the corner and hurling it across the sterile room. "Over. We begin again."

She didn't answer. She simply stared at him with her too bright eyes and her full mouth that hadn't smiled in hours.

Suddenly Anabella couldn't bear another moment of conversation. She didn't want to hear another thing. Didn't want to ask another question. She was overwhelmed and needed time to digest what he'd told her. She needed quiet to deal with her emotions.

"It's late, isn't it?" she said, glancing to the window and the dark night, feeling dangerously close to tears but these were tears she didn't understand. She should have been overjoyed that she and Lucio were married. She'd always wanted to be his wife. So why didn't she feel joy? Why was there no relief?

"Not too long until dinner."

Ana turned away, closed her eyes, held back the hot gritty tears. "I'm rather worn out," she said, struggling to keep her voice neutral. "Would you mind if I just had dinner alone in my room tonight?"

He hesitated and she looked at him over her shoulder. His features were hard, closed. He looked nearly as upset as she felt.

And yet when he answered her, he sounded very calm. Deceptively relaxed. "No, of course not. We'll do whatever you want, *carida*. We'll do whatever you need."

Lucio had dinner alone downstairs on the veranda. He ate in the dark, with just candles on the table to illuminate his meal.

The silent dinner by candlelight reminded him of his old life, the life he'd left behind, the life where he'd been so free. He'd had few responsibilities as a gaucho. No commitments. No obligations. He came, he went, he did as he pleased.

And then came Anabella and he traded the freedom for a life with her. He gave up the things he'd enjoyed for things she'd recognize; money, power, social position. She'd come from those things. He'd assumed she needed those things still.

Lucio lit a small cigar at the end of his meal and held the fragrant burning cigar to his nose. He didn't like to smoke very much but he loved the aroma of fine dried tobacco.

The scent of tobacco reminded him of friends, his father, his brother. Reminded him of the nights he slept alone beneath the stars. Reminded him of the campfires, the round-ups, the long days herding cattle, branding, riding hard across the plains.

He'd loved his life in the mountains, and he'd loved his life on the pampas, and that life had pleased him. Fulfilled him. Until Ana.

Lucio crushed out the burning tip of the cigar and pushed away from the table. Entering his big stone and plaster villa he found it painfully ironic that he, who'd never had anything growing up, now had everything. And he, who'd never wanted anything until Anabella, didn't have her.

The house was dark. Lucio had sat outside so long that even Maria had turned off the lights in the kitchen and gone home.

Lucio locked the front door, locked the back door and

climbed the curving staircase to the second floor. And yet as he climbed the stairs he felt increasingly aware of Anabella.

In so many ways they were two halves of a whole. And being half of a whole, he knew Ana was lonely right now.

He stood at the top of the stairs on the dark landing and knew he couldn't go to bed without speaking to her. His conscience wouldn't allow it.

His heart forbid it.

Quietly he opened her bedroom door. Her room was dark and the moon outside shone dimly, an outline of yellow and gold from behind a high thick cloud.

He saw her curled on her side in the big bed. She didn't move and she didn't speak to him but her eyes were open and she was watching him.

"I wanted to say I'm sorry if I hurt you." He cleared his throat. "Forgive me, Anabella."

"What is there to forgive?"

Her flippant tone didn't fool him. Her voice sounded hoarse, husky. She'd been crying earlier.

He moved towards the bed. She lifted the covers up, pulling them over her head. She was able to hide everything but the ten little fingers clutching the sheet.

He couldn't help smiling. They were very cute little fingers.

He wanted her to put the sheet down. He wanted to see her pretty face. Leaning over, he kissed one finger and then another and another. Her fingers tightened on the sheet, her knuckles went white.

She was so stubborn.

Lightly, with the tip of his tongue, he touched one white knuckle. She gasped. He smiled faintly before covering the entire knuckle with his mouth. He sucked on it gently, and then harder, almost rhythmically. As he sucked her knuckle he saw her squirm beneath the covers.

He gave the same attention to the rest of her fingers, but still Anabella kept hidden.

He stood, headed for the door. "Well, good night."

"Don't go."

He turned around. She was sitting up in bed now. The room was so dark it was hard to see her but he could make out her wide eyes, the pensive set of her jaw.

"We're really *married*," she said.

"Yes."

"How long ago did we marry?"

"It's been a couple of years now." The dark room grew even dimmer. He looked towards the window. A silver rimmed cloud had moved in front of the moon. The night was late and the tension Lucio felt seemed to wrap the room itself.

"Why didn't you tell me sooner?" Her voice was but a whisper.

"Because you weren't yourself. When I returned here, when your family called me, you were very emotional. Very fragile."

Her watched her brow furrow as she struggled to take it all in.

"And this is our house, isn't it?" she asked, lightly running her hand across the burgundy silk coverlet.

"Yes."

She touched the luxurious fabric again. "It doesn't feel like our house. I can't imagine us really living here."

"We've been here almost four years."

Her lips parted, but no sound came out.

He could see the bewilderment in her eyes, feel her confusion. "You still don't remember very much, do you?"

She shook her head. "I've spent the whole evening trying to remember but I can't. I can't see anything in my head. I can't picture anything."

"I have more pictures, photos from our wedding. I'll get it if you like—"

"No. Not tonight. I can't bear to think. I can't stand feeling so...empty."

She sounded so exhausted and she looked so small in the

big bed that once was their bed. He wanted to wrap her in his arms and keep her safe. "I'm sorry, *negrita.*"

Her saw her lower lip quivered. He'd give anything to kiss her mouth, to make the quiver go away. "I'm sorry if I hurt you. You know I never wanted to hurt you."

"Then come here. Hold me."

Lucio drew a deep breath. He wanted to hold her. He wanted to hold her more than anything but he didn't trust himself. She needed tenderness and yet he needed her. He was afraid to touch her, afraid he couldn't control his hunger to be close to her.

It'd been forever since they last made love. Months and months—longer than he cared to admit.

"I can't," he said, needing words, knowing he had to stop this, had to contain the need before it got out of control. "Why?"

"Because I don't know that I could keep my hands off you."

"Then don't."

Just those two little words from her and he felt a blaze of desire sweep through him, a need so strong that he felt ruthless. Dangerous.

Back away, he told himself. But he couldn't move. It felt as if hot honey filled his veins.

The hot honey was Ana, the hot honey was wanting to be inside Ana. His body hurt. His groin ached. If he wasn't careful he'd pull her beneath him, fill her completely, bury himself deep where he felt most at home.

"You said we're married."

He smothered a groan. "But it's been a long time—"

"Well, *you* were the one that came to see *me.*"

Her voice floated at him in the dark. He could barely see her, but he felt her. One touch, he told himself. He wanted just one touch.

But they weren't together anymore, and she didn't remember. She'd been the one to divorce him. She'd wanted something else, he reminded himself, and yet she was waiting for him now.

Loving Anabella was excruciating. Leaving Anabella impossible.

"Stay," her husky voice entreated in the darkness. "I won't bite."

He almost laughed but the emotion felt raw. "Yes, you will." She'd often bite him when they made love. She'd scratched, too.

Scars he'd once worn proudly. Scars that had healed and faded. It'd been too long since they'd been wild together. Too long since they made such hot fierce savage love.

So long since he'd made any kind of love.

"Ana." His voice was pitched so low, and so full of hunger, it hurt his own ears.

"Come see me," she whispered.

He'd been insane to come here. He'd tried so hard to stay away from her. "You've been through a lot, Ana. You're still not very strong."

He hated how tight his slacks felt. He hated how tight his skin felt. His skin couldn't contain him. His body would betray him.

He heard the rustle of fabric, the sensuous slide of silk against silk. She'd left the bed and was moving towards him. He saw a glimmer of gold and then she was before him, hovering just a breath away.

"You're so stubborn," she softly mocked. "You're so determined to be good, but I'm sick of being good. I've been good my whole life and it's the most boring thing imaginable."

This was the vamp and vixen of his heart. "You've *never* been good."

"Thank God." She laughed a little, the sound sexy, so damn sexy. "I'd hate to be boring."

He was drowning. He was drowning beneath the weight of the thousands of hungry dreams he'd had over the past few lonely months.

"Touch me, Lucio."

"I can't."

"You can. Only you can make me feel like me, and I want to feel like me again."

He was Adam in the garden of Eden. He was reaching for the apple, dying for the apple, wanted the apple more than he'd wanted anything in his life. It would be so good. It'd taste so good—

"No." He groaned the word, the cry pulled from him, the pain as intense as if someone had reached in and pulled out his heart. "I can't do this, Ana."

He knew she'd never forgive him if he made love to her with her memory shot and her world half gone. He knew the Anabella that had divorced him had been so full of resentment and contempt.

God, he hated being good. It was so not him.

Her arms wrapped around his waist. Her hands knotted in his lower back. She pressed her cheek against his chest. "Don't be a coward," she teased, lifting her face.

"I'm not."

The moon slid from behind a cloud illuminating the sky in a wash of white and silver light.

In the sudden brightness he saw Anabella's face clearly, her wide green eyes dark with emotion and passion. Unable to help himself, unable to resist such beautiful eyes and beautiful lips, he brushed his mouth against hers and breathed her in.

I love you, he thought, the faint pressure of his lips drawing a tremor from her. *I love you, Anabella, from here until eternity. I'll love you all the way from one ocean to another.* And her body trembled against his.

She was begging him to hold her, to put his arms around her, but the very thing she craved would be his undoing.

Slowly he ended the kiss and even more slowly he lifted his head. Her lashes flickered. Her eyes opened. She was staring up at him and in the soft white light he saw the sparkle of tears in her eyes.

"You used to love kissing me." Her voice sounded so young, so confused, the voice of innocence.

He wanted to kiss the tears from her eyes. He wanted to hold her face in his hands and love away the sadness, and the pain, and the confusion of a life shattered into different pieces. But she needed stability and reality, more than she needed a fantasy world with him. "I still do."

"But you don't want me?"

Oh, chica, I want you, but I have to protect you. Even if it means protecting you from me.

He stroked her cheek with his thumb.. "Remember how sick you've been. Your body is still recovering."

She made an indignant sound. "I'm recovered. Look at me," and she lifted her arms up, the moonlight bathing her gleaming skin and the high fullness of her breasts. "I'm perfectly healthy."

Yes, her body looked perfectly healthy. Her body also looked perfectly beautiful. He couldn't take his eyes off her breasts and the taut outline of her nipples against the thin gold silk nightgown.

He could imagine the gown slipped off her shoulders and the flat stretch of her belly and the triangle of dark curls at the juncture of her thighs. He loved the darkness of the curls against the paleness of her skin. He loved the different textures—smooth, crisp, silk, slick.

Women were so beautifully made and none more lovely than Anabella. And he wanted her in his arms, wanted her naked against him, beneath him. He wanted her breast in his mouth, his hands on her hips, his body deep inside hers.

But it wasn't going to happen.

"Good night, Anabella." He forced himself to smile to ease the shaft of pain inside him. "I'll see you in the morning."

Inside his room, Lucio pressed his forehead against the door, body rippling with need, heart aching with loss. It was his dream to be with her again. He had a terrible need to merge with her, to close the distance between them. But he couldn't.

Count to ten, he told himself, grinding the words into his mind to keep from thinking about the hard heat in his body. *Count to ten and then to twenty and if that doesn't work, start all over.*

CHAPTER SEVEN

ANABELLA woke early after a fitful night's sleep. She'd tossed and turned and dreamed wild, lurid dreams and yet woken frustrated and exhausted.

Why?

Because her gaucho husband wouldn't touch her! Not only that, he'd practically run out of the bedroom last night. What was that all about?

And why were they sleeping in separate rooms? This whole situation was not right. She wanted Lucio. She knew he wanted her. They'd always had a great physical relationship. It was time they had one again.

Ana tossed back the covers to go shower. At least she had a goal for the day.

Ana met Lucio downstairs as he prepared to sit down for breakfast. "You're up early," he said, rising to hold her chair for her.

She sat down across from him and smiled at Maria who brought her a coffee and *alfajor*, a crumbly biscuit filled with caramel and bathed in chocolate. "I've decided I must get back into a regular routine." She added a heaping spoon of sugar to her *café cortado*, a dark espresso cut with steamed milk. "Especially if I hope to get my *strength* back."

She saw Lucio look at her hard as she emphasized the word strength.

"I must make sure I'm fully *recovered*." And with a sweet smile at Lucio she took a small bite of her caramel stuffed pastry. The caramel was sticky and very sweet and she felt some cling to her upper lip. She knew he was watching her closely. And daintily, with the tip of her tongue, she licked off the creamy caramel from her lip.

Lifting the pastry between two fingers, she looked at him over the chocolate covered top. "I don't want to be sick anymore." And carefully, very carefully, she opened her mouth and slid the pastry between her lips.

Lucio made a rough sound in the back of his throat.

Ana purred. "Mmm. Delicious." And wiping her fingers off on her linen napkin, she picked up her coffee and pushed away from the table.

She flashed a quick smile, loved his grim expression. "Have a good day at the office, Lucio. Hope to see you tonight."

And she hoped that he'd burn all day for her the same way she'd burned last night.

Lucio indeed spent a restless day in his office, and the restlessness only increased as the sun grew warmer, hotter. He took off his jacket and unbuttoned his shirt but Lucio couldn't get cool.

He tried distracting himself with phone calls but he only wanted to hear Ana's voice.

It's just the heat, he told himself, irritably closing his blinds but even in the semi-dark he found himself thinking of Anabella. He could see her as she was last night, body warm and sensuous in her gold nightgown. He could see her at breakfast with the creamy caramel *dulce de leche* on her lips and practically feel the tip of her pink tongue as it slowly licked the sticky sweetness from her mouth.

God, he wanted her. He'd never stopped wanting her. He was a masochist to be sleeping every night in the same house with her.

Lucio pushed away from the desk, angry, disgusted. What *was* he doing back at the villa? Why had he agreed to return? She'd sent him away. Her family had shut the door on him. And yet the moment things started to fall apart, the

Galváns called for him, wanted him to come in and fix Anabella.

Fix Anabella! As if that was his job.

As if he'd ever say no.

Lucio leaned against the desk, closed his eyes, tried to see a way clear of the disastrous situation he'd gotten himself in.

Breakfast with Anabella. Dinner with Anabella. Walks in the moonlight with Anabella. Kisses at midnight with Anabella.

Go ahead, he told himself. Quit fighting it. Jump. You might as well give up. She's got you. She owns you. Now and forever.

He returned to the villa late but Ana greeted him at the door, wearing tight jeans, high heeled boots and a snug white T-shirt that showed off the full curves of her breasts.

She wasn't wearing a bra, he saw, and her dark nipples were outlined *perfectly*.

Hell and damnation. He was cursed.

"Would you like a drink?" she asked, taking his coat, smiling sweetly as if she'd been made expressly for this task of waiting at the door to meet and greet.

"No." It was a surly reply but it was honest.

"*Hard* day?" she asked with another innocent smile but he heard the way she hit the word hard, heard the hint of laughter in her voice.

"Not too bad."

"Nothing *urgent* or *pressing*?"

Like his aching arousal? "*No.*" He glared at her. He'd make her pay. He would. He'd tie her up and kiss her senseless.

No. She'd enjoy that too much.

Footsteps sounded in the hallway behind them. "Dinner will be served an hour from now," Maria, the housekeeper announced.

"Not a problem," Ana answered cheerfully, handing

Maria Lucio's coat. "This will give the Senor and I a little time to...relax...together."

The housekeeper folded the coat over her arm and disappeared.

"I somehow don't think anything you plan will be relaxing," he said darkly as Ana led him into the elegant living room she'd decorated and furnished herself.

Together they entered the spacious room with the antiques, and oil paintings, and delicately carved folding screen.

She flashed him a wicked smile as her fingers brushed the back of the chaise longue upholstered in a persimmon colored textile. "Afraid of being alone with me?"

Her smile beat at him.

The little imp. Still such a vixen. It was so hard being with her like this. He was finding it increasingly difficult to manage his emotions. How could he possibly hide his love, his hurt, his need?

She didn't know what they'd been through this year.

He followed after her more slowly. "No, not afraid of you. Maybe I'm afraid for you. You're such a fragile little thing—"

"Please, Senor," she interrupted, leaning against the back of the chaise, her eyes glinting with mischief. "Don't turn this into a wrestling match. I have a couple of moves that would quickly immobilize you."

"That would be some trick, *negrita*," he answered indulgently, amused by her humor. She'd never change. She'd be impossible until the day she died.

"Is that a dare?" she answered, moving slowly toward him, provocation sparkling in her green eyes.

She wanted to play, wanted fire, and Lucio's amusement gave way to incredulity as she stopped in front of him and reached out to run a hand up his thigh, over his hip.

His breath caught in his throat. His body went hot and hard. He couldn't have made a move if he tried.

"*Senor,* you were saying?" Her hand settled at his crotch, lovingly cupping him and he nearly burst from his skin.

"*Ana,*" he growled, grabbing her hand.

"*Sí, Senor?*"

"Stop it with the Senor stuff." He lifted her hand, kissed her palm, fought the urge to kiss every finger and between every finger.

Fought the urge to put her hand right back on his groin.

His mood—as well as the night—was no longer quite as cool and calm as a moment ago. Lucio felt hot. Very hot and he was close to doing something he'd regret. "Maybe we should take a walk, or get out a deck of cards—"

"You hate cards."

"I know, but you used to like them."

"Yes. If we're playing strip poker."

"Ana, you're supposed to be resting. Relaxing. Taking things easy."

She grinned. "I'm easy."

Jesus! She was going to drive him mad.

He turned away, pressed a knuckle fist to his temple. *Relax,* he told himself. *She's just playing. She's just trying to liven things up a little.*

And a voice inside him answered darkly, *Oh yes, she's livened things up more than a little.*

Suddenly she laughed. "Come on, Lucio. Laugh. Have fun with me. Can't we still have fun together?"

She reached out, wrapped her arms around one of his. "Lucio," she whispered, eyebrows arching, "it's just me!"

"That's what I'm afraid of."

Her eyes met his and her eyebrows arched and then she laughed again, a lower, huskier laugh. She knew exactly what he was thinking, and from the way she pressed her hips against his, rubbing lightly, very suggestively, she knew exactly what he was feeling because she was feeling it, too.

Ana broke away and moved to the red, lacquered cabinet outfitted on the inside with a complete bar, including ice and a mini refrigerator, and he watched her suffused with need and hunger. She made him ache. She made him burn. And she loved it.

"You found the bar," he said, still struggling to get his breathing under control as she opened the doors on the shiny red cabinet. Two years ago Ana had lined the interior of the cabinet with mirror and added a small halogen spotlight and all the glass and mirror surfaces sparkled.

She hesitated before the staggering display of bottles, decanters and crystal glasses. "Maria took me on a tour of the house and then I spent the afternoon exploring on my own," she answered suddenly distracted. "But I realize I don't know what you drink."

He didn't immediately answer, too fascinated by her, enjoying just looking at her. He loved the way her long hair swept her cheek, the small of her back, the generous curve of hip. Women were like beautiful undulating waves, and no one had a sweeter shape than Anabella.

She glanced at him over her shoulder. "What do you like?"

You. But he didn't say it. He swallowed the hot surge of desire and the wildness of his emotions. She made him feel so fierce, so alive and it'd been forever since he burned like this. "Red wine."

She stared into the cabinet. "We don't keep wine here, do we?"

"No. There's a wine cellar downstairs." He saw her look of surprise and the impersonal conversation was good, he thought. Talking about ordinary things gave him time to check his desire, focus on important things—like her health. "I take it you didn't discover the cellar?"

"No." She slowly shut the cabinet doors. "It's a big house."

"You decorated it yourself."

"I did?" Her brow furrowed as she took in the formal room. "So what do you do? And how did we pay for all

BUSINESS REPLY MAIL
FIRST-CLASS MAIL   PERMIT NO. 717-003   BUFFALO, NY

POSTAGE WILL BE PAID BY ADDRESSEE

HARLEQUIN READER SERVICE
3010 WALDEN AVE
PO BOX 1867
BUFFALO NY 14240-9952

NO POSTAGE
NECESSARY
IF MAILED
IN THE
UNITED STATES

this?'' Her gesture included the furniture, the art, the house itself.

''I've been successful. You have an antique business.''

An antique business, she silently repeated, trying to digest the information. ''It's hard to believe. I don't feel it…I don't feel like this. None of it's familiar.''

''It'll start coming back to you, Ana. It already has.''

But there was no elation in his voice, nothing joyous at all, and her heart sank. ''Were we happy, Lucio?''

He stood perfectly still and for a moment Ana wasn't sure he was going to answer, increasingly unnerved by his silence.

Slowly his lips curved and his dark eyes burned and she thought he looked like an angel on fire.

''What do you think?'' he answered softly.

The intensity in his eyes made her inhale. He burned for her. He loved her. She was sure of that much. But there was something else happening between them, something that wasn't patient, it wasn't gentle, and it wasn't kind.

She felt her throat constrict. ''We didn't have a good marriage, did we?''

His jaw tightened. ''It wasn't all bad.''

''When was it good?''

His silence frightened her. *''Lucio.''*

His teeth clicked as he clenched his jaw. He looked almost tortured.

''When were we happy?'' she persisted.

His eyes held hers. ''When we were in bed.''

His words stayed with Ana as she changed out of her jeans and into something more elegant for the late dinner that was customary in her country.

Ana put on a delicate red chiffon dress embroidered with black beaded flowers and brushed her hair before tying it in a loose knot at her nape. She added gold hoop earrings and a hint of perfume behind her ears, at her wrists, and behind her knees.

Lucio waited for her outside the formal dining room with the gleaming bronze walls. It was the first time they had eaten together in the dining room and she liked how dramatic it looked at night with the lights dimmed and candles flickering on the table and the long serpentine console.

Before dinner was served, Lucio put some music on so they could listen to it during their meal.

Maria was a magnificent cook and she'd prepared an assortment of Italian dishes, a favorite of Anabella's. After their plates were cleared Ana and Lucio moved back into the living room to have their coffee where they could enjoy the music even better.

Ana curled her legs beneath her as she sipped her coffee. Despite her rather fuzzy sense of reality, she felt happy. How was such a thing possible?

Maybe it was because she wasn't allowing herself to look too far ahead. She wasn't thinking about the future, or the journey she knew lay ahead.

Like finding her son.

There was time for everything, she told herself, and right now, she simply wanted to enjoy tonight with Lucio.

Bringing the small china cup to her mouth, Anabella felt the porcelain's smooth edge, the heat of the cup, smelled the rich aroma of freshly brewed espresso. Such little pleasures, she thought, and yet these little pleasures combined with Lucio's close proximity were heady. Almost decadent. She felt as if she'd been given the entire world.

"You're so beautiful, Anabella."

Lucio's deep voice sent a prickle of sensation down her spine followed by a rush of pleasure. It was as if he'd touched her with the tip of his finger.

She lifted her head, gazed at him and he stared at her for a long silent moment, as if life was suspended and she belonged to no world but his. It was the very thing she'd found so attractive in the beginning, back before she even knew his name. That quiet watchful presence, that sense that he knew things she'd never know, that feeling of being wanted simply because she was.

It had never been about accomplishment, she thought, never about family, money, connections. It—the attraction—was pure energy. Intangible, invisible, addictive.

"We still have much to discuss," Lucio said quietly, placing his espresso cup on the table next to him. "There's more I need to tell you."

She felt a tender pang. She was certain the "more" wouldn't be good.

"Can it wait until tomorrow?" she asked, knowing she was just avoiding the inevitable.

He smiled faintly. "You and Scarlett O'Hara could have been twins."

Her heart ached. It was true. She'd always been so good at procrastinating, avoiding, pretending. Ana had always preferred fantasy to reality.

"You know me too well," she said, feeling an overwhelming love for Lucio, realizing that their lives had been intertwined for many years now. Maybe she didn't remember it all in her head, but she felt connected to him in her heart.

"Which is why we have to talk, Ana. Part of me doesn't want to talk, a big part of me would rather continue like this." His dark eyes were almost smoky with silent secret emotion. "But this, you and me together like this... We haven't been close like this in years."

Her eyes held his. "Then maybe this is just what we need."

"Living in denial? No, I don't think so."

"Maybe it's not living in denial. Maybe…maybe we have a second chance at love. A chance to get it right this time."

He briefly closed his eyes. "That's the tricky part, *negrita*. It's always been right for me." His eyes opened and the shadows were deeper, more haunted. "You have been unhappy with me. You've wanted out of our marriage for a long time."

Ana wanted to cover her ears. She didn't like this, didn't want to hear this. This talk would make her sad and she didn't want to be sad tonight. It was a gorgeous night. The evening air was still warm and the French doors were open welcoming the scent of fragrant spring flowers into the house.

No. They weren't going to talk. No reason to talk. They were together. That's all that mattered. And for now, that was all she needed to know.

Ana rose from her chair and walked to his side. She stood above him, one hand on her hip, the other extended out to him. "Dance with me."

"*Ana.*"

"What? We don't dance anymore?" She arched a fine black eyebrow. "You can't tell me we never danced. You like to dance. You're a very good dancer." Her other brow lifted. "Or have I mixed that up, too?"

She watched the struggle on his face, watched the brief emotion cross, hunger, desire, need. Like last night, he wanted her. And like last night, he was afraid. He was afraid to touch her. Why?

His smile was small but deadly and so very very sexy. "I like to dance. You haven't forgotten."

"Mmm." She felt the heat inside her, and the elusive happiness she'd once known with him. And she remembered in a bright hot flash, that it'd been so intense between them. Their love had been like a firestorm.

Heaven and hell.

"Then show me," she murmured, reaching down to take his hand in hers, her fingers lacing with his.

She felt his pulse jump, felt his skin grow warm every place their hands touched. The energy between them was so sharp it almost hurt. She hadn't remembered that it felt like this to touch. She hadn't remembered that the pleasure was edged with pain.

The song playing on the stereo was slow, a sultry song

by a female singer that seemed to grow the night around them, snug and tight.

Lucio tucked her hand behind his back, bringing her all the way against him, her breasts against his chest, her hips cradled against his. He was taller than she remembered, and her head fit neatly against his chest, her cheek against his heart but it wasn't a comforting feeling, wasn't calming. She felt on fire. She felt skewered and seared, like *asado* on the grill.

"Your heart's racing," he said. "And we haven't even started dancing yet."

She felt the rasp of his thumb across the inside of her wrist. He was taking her pulse. The arrogant man. "I'm perfectly fine."

His dark head bent, his eyes meeting hers, his expression intense. "Yes, you are."

Her heart pounded even harder. Her mouth went dry. He was looking at her as if she were the sweetest dish of ice cream. All French vanilla with sweet cherries on top. Now if only he'd use his tongue to lick her from top to bottom.

"You're smiling," he said, head bending lower, his lips brushing the top of her hair. "Why?"

His breath tickled her forehead and she could almost feel his kiss against her skin. He was so big, so muscular. She shivered and he pressed her closer to his frame. "I was just thinking I didn't forget this."

He inhaled and she felt his ribs expand. She felt the shape of his body against her and it was delicious. It was amazing to feel like a woman again.

"Neither did I," he murmured. His dark head dipped and his mouth caressed her cheek, a slow tender kiss that made the nerves scream up and down her spine.

She swallowed, her mouth still dry, her pulse pounding. She lifted one hand to his hair, "Hare you always worn your hair long?"

Creases fanned from his eyes. He was smiling a little, but

the expression in the dark depths was anything but sweet. "Always."

He kissed her, near the corner of her mouth. "You wouldn't let me cut it," he added softly in her ear, his tongue tracing the outer curve of her ear and then the delicate inner shell. "You said you wouldn't make love to me if I ever wore it short."

She gasped a little at the caress of his tongue. Her body ached everywhere, but the strongest ache was in her belly, between her thighs. She wanted him and she knew he wanted her and the blatant sexual energy nearly knocked her off her feet.

"Let's go upstairs." She brushed her lips across his chin, felt the sharp rasp of beard. "Let's go upstairs and just be together."

Lucio felt her small mouth open, her teeth nibble at his chin. Her tongue, warm and damp, traced invisible lines down his throat and his body felt so hard, so hot, he was desperate to get out of his jeans.

But that didn't mean he could. "I can't, Ana." His hands covered her bare shoulders, his hands sliding across her smooth silky skin. He felt her collarbone, the base of her slim throat, the soft hair at her nape. "I don't trust myself alone with you."

And it crossed his mind that he'd always feel this way about her. He'd never be able to be around her and not want her. He'd never not feel the shimmering need. It burned so hot now, it was like being burned alive.

"Not that old story again." Ana took his hands in hers and pressed his palms to her ribs before sliding his hands up to cup her breasts.

He groaned deep in his throat. She wasn't wearing a bra and his hands were filled with the sweet firmness of her breasts. He couldn't do this again. Couldn't fight himself again. Last night he'd used all his willpower up.

"Ana," he growled, *you are torturing me.*

"Yes *mi amor?*" Her lips were warm at his throat. Her nails lightly raked his chest.

His body tensed, jerked, his erection so powerful it hurt. He couldn't hold out. He couldn't refuse her two nights in a row.

Impatiently he pushed the scoop neckline further off her shoulders, pushing the fabric down to expose her full pale breasts. She looked gorgeous. Her breasts gleamed and her nipples had hardened into small tight buds.

Arching her backward, he covered one taut nipple with his mouth and the other with his hand. He felt like a man starving. He was famished. He drew her breast into his mouth, sucked on the exquisite nipple, felt her shudder in his arms and he lapped his tongue over and around the peak, unable to get enough of her, unable to answer his hunger.

He reached beneath her dress, traced the shape of her thigh, caught the firm cheek of her bottom in his hand. He kneaded the flesh, his fingers, knuckles, palms pressing into her skin, and as he touched her, he felt her heat, felt her tremble against him.

She wanted him.

Lucio closed his eyes, let his hand go where it hadn't been able to go in so long. Beneath her skirt, beneath her small silky thong, he felt her softness, the core of her hot and wet. He slid a finger into her, heard her cry out against his shoulder and he withdrew from her, afraid of hurting her, afraid of letting this get too far.

Trembling she pressed herself closer to him. "Touch me again, Lucio. Make me feel good again."

And there was no way he could not touch her now, no way to keep his hands off her or keep his lips from kissing the pulse beating at the base of her ear. He kissed her pulse, kissed her neck, kissed her mouth.

Ana moaned as he slid her thong panties to one side and pressed a finger into her, and then two, thrusting in and out the way he would have with his body.

Ana cried against his chest, her lips finding warm bare

skin. He was touching her in a way she hadn't been touched in a very long time, and instead of calming the need, it was setting her on fire, making her crave more.

This wasn't enough, she thought blindly. She wanted all of him, wanted to feel his muscles, his strength, every bit of his skin. "Upstairs," she panted, her teeth against the firm muscle of his chest. "Let's go upstairs. Now. Please. Right now."

Lucio reluctantly pulled away, adjusted her thong, making sure the fine silky line of panty fit perfectly at the cleft of her derriere. He settled the skirt of her dress over her hips and adjusted the neckline off her shoulders again.

He was breathing hard, Ana heard his hoarse breathing and she kissed him. "We're not done yet," she said, kissing him again.

They went upstairs, Ana leading, Lucio following, and it hurt him to move, his body so rock hard.

He ached for her. He wanted her more than he'd ever wanted anyone. There was a big world out there—millions of women—and he only wanted one. Only needed one.

This one.

Ana felt the chemistry between them. They weren't speaking but the connection was so strong, the intensity almost overpowering.

It was hot between them. Hot and explosive. But was it love they felt? Or was it hate?

She glanced back over her shoulder at Lucio.

Love—she thought looking back at his mouth, knowing what it could do to her, knowing she loved what he could to her.

Or hate. And her gaze shifted to his eyes where the expression was already remote. One wouldn't have known that he'd just been kissing her, intimately touching her, giving her such pleasure.

At the door of her bedroom she faced him. His dark eyes met hers and she saw a flash in the deep brown eyes. "Is there somewhere else you want to be tonight?" she asked, her voice husky in the dark. They hadn't turned the hall light on and the only light was the reflection of the moon shining through the oval-shaped second floor window.

"No."

She smiled a little and yet the smile made her throat close up and chest feel raw. "Is there someone else you want to be with?"

His long dark hair fell forward, half shading his face. "Never."

Never. Good answer. She swallowed her smile. "I want you to love me tonight, Lucio. I want you to love me the way you once loved me." Her eyes held his. "Please."

"I can't, Anabella. You've been sick—"

"No, no, come up with something new, Lucio! I'm so bored of that line."

He bent his head. She saw that his eyes were closed. His features looked knotted with pain.

A lump formed in her throat and gently she touched his mouth and then his cheek, his beard bristling against her hand. "This is hard for you, too, isn't it?"

"I'm so afraid of hurting you. I want you, *negrita*, but I'd never forgive myself if I accidentally hurt you."

She swallowed the disappointment. Her heart understood even if her body didn't. "Then don't make love to me. Just stay. Sleep with me—"

"It'll never happen. I won't be able to keep my hands off you."

"You won't have to. You can hold me." Her green eyes flashed with naughty intent. "You just can't get too excited."

CHAPTER EIGHT

THEY silently undressed in the dark and slipped beneath the covers, Lucio in just his boxers and Ana her gold chemise. In bed she curled against his side, his chest a pillow for her head.

For a long moment they didn't speak, then Ana turned in Lucio's arms to see him better.

She loved the way the moonlight edged his face, and made his dark eyes glow. Lucio was one of those people who were beautiful in the day but at night he seemed to truly come alive. It must be his Indian blood, she thought, that and his birth high in the rugged mountains. Lucio had always loved the mountains.

"Remember the night we slept outside, beneath the stars?" She lightly caressed the smooth taut muscle wrapping his rib cage. "Remember how still everything was?"

"Yes." His hand covered the top of her head. She felt his fingers slide through her hair, separating the strands, combing out the tangles.

"We could see thousands of stars that night," she added. "We could see the shadow of the mountains, and the moon. That night it was like we were the only ones alive."

"It was beautiful," he agreed.

"I wish it could be that way again. I wish we could feel that way together again."

"And how did we feel?"

"Safe."

He didn't say anything, he just kept stroking her hair as she continued talking. "At least, I think it felt safe. I'm not sure. As you know, the past is sort of hazy, almost like a dream. Sometimes I wonder if we're real. If any of this is real—'' she broke off, drew a deep breath and curled closer to him, her cheek pressed to his warm chest.

"But then when I touch you, and feel you, and have you hold me like this," and her hand touched his heart, "I know it's okay. *We're* okay."

Eyes closed, she put her lips to his chest, drank in the spicy scent of his skin. The planes of his chest were endless, his torso smooth and long. She caressed his stomach with her fingertips and felt the muscles in his belly clench. He felt so good to her. He felt the way home felt. "I know I've been sick, and I know I've forgotten five years of my life, but whatever has come between us, Lucio, whatever has created this...mistrust...I think we can work it out."

He made a soft hoarse sound. "But Ana, if you can't remember the problem you had with me, how can we fix it?"

"Maybe the problem wasn't with you. Maybe I had a problem with me. Either way, there's no reason we can't try again. Never mind the old memories. We'll make new ones." She sat up, leaned on her elbow. "I mean, doesn't this feel so right...us being together like this?"

The corner of his mouth curved. "You're so damn optimistic."

"How about you?" she asked, looking down at him. "Ready for an adventure?"

"Oh, Ana—"

"No, don't do that. Think like a gaucho, Lucio. Let's run away together. Make a new life together. Just you and me."

"Where do you want to go?"

"Doesn't matter as long as we're together."

"And what would we do?"

She felt a flash of irritation. Lucio had grown so...weary, so serious. He'd become so preoccupied with details. What had happened to his wild free spirit?

"Uh-oh," he said, "I know that look. There's a storm coming." His deep voice moved across her like the hot wind across the sun-bleached pampas and his fingertips rubbed soft circles at her temple. "I can feel the energy here."

She tried to smile. "When did you become such an old man?"

"Maybe when I realized I was going to lose you." His hands tightened on her arms and he pulled her against him, close to his chest. "I didn't like it at all."

She could smell his soap, his spicy aftershave, and the warm musky scent of his skin. He smelled familiar, and felt familiar. "You know, I don't remember being unwell."

"You don't have to. You're much better now. That's all that's important."

She turned her face against his chest, felt the hair on his hard chest rasp her cheek, his nipple brush her lips. "You weren't here when I went to the hospital, were you?"

"No. You caught the illness in China, probably from a mosquito bite, and it wasn't diagnosed until you'd returned home."

"And where were you?"

"France. Then California."

She swallowed. Lucio had been to France, and the States. "For business?"

"The winery, yes."

"And when did they send for you?"

"Not until they realized how much you needed me. Once I heard you were ill, I came right away."

"And my mother?" she whispered. "Has she been to see me?" But the moment Ana asked the question, she knew the answer. No. Of course her mother hadn't come. Her mother wouldn't. "Never mind. Don't answer that. I know Mama hasn't."

She drew a deep shuddering breath, her head tingling with that strange prickly sensation it seemed to get now. "As much as I love Dante, he's not my family anymore. You're my family. You're the only one who matters—"

"Ana, we're not married." He said the words swiftly as he sat up, the sheet falling to his hips.

"What do you mean we're not married anymore? This is our house. You're a vintner. I sell antiques."

"It happened."

"What happened? *Divorce?*"

She saw him nod and her stomach heaved. "We found each other after two years, we married, and then we divorced?"

"Pretty much sums it up."

"No!" Her disbelief echoed in the moonlit bedroom. This was not possible. This she absolutely could not accept. "So if we're divorced, where do you live?"

"I have an apartment in downtown Mendoza."

"It can't be! I'd never do that—we'd never do that—" she broke off, too stunned for words.

Lucio's lips compressed and he stared at her with those dark, secretive eyes of his.

She felt a welling of rage. "Say something! Tell me how this came to be."

"I don't have all the answers."

"Well, what answers do you have?" Her chest felt tight, she fought to get enough air. He couldn't be right. They were in love. They were meant to be together. They would always be together. "Did you fall in love with someone else?"

"The divorce wasn't my idea." Lucio made a low rough sound in his throat. "I wish I could say there was some other woman, but this wasn't me, this wasn't my decision, this wasn't what I wanted at all."

"Well, I didn't want it!"

"Yes you did," he told her softly. "And you got it because I wanted you to be happy."

She shook her head. Her heart raced so fast she couldn't breathe and her head hurt, sharp pain grinding at the front of her skull between her temples. "Happy to be away from you? That's not possible! You're making this up."

"You don't remember."

Her eyes welled with tears. "I'd remember something like that."

"You haven't yet, but you will. It's all starting to come back to you, the pieces, the fragments. It might take a few days, another couple weeks, but sooner or later you'll remember."

They faced each other over a void as great as the Patagonia glaciers. Her eyes were gritty and her body felt cold. She was going to cry and she had a horrible sense that she was freezing on the inside, freezing into one of the famous glaciers, and like them, she might never thaw. "I *do* love you, Lucio."

"But not enough, Ana." He said the words so tenderly they nearly broke her heart.

She wrapped her arms around him, buried her face against his chest. "Forgive me, Lucio. Forgive me. Give me another chance. Let's make this work."

He stroked the back of her head. "But we don't even know why it didn't work this last time. I think we need answers before we can make any commitments."

She was crying, crying hard, in earnest and he lay back down and carried her with him. "It's going to be all right, Anabella. You're going to have a great life—"

"Not if it's without you!"

She sounded so passionate, so stricken, and the vulnerability in her voice touched his heart.

"I can't stand this," she wept. "I can't stand these huge gaps in my memory, can't stand that you know everything while I grope in the dark, struggling to just put faces with names!"

"It's slowly coming back," he comforted, rolling her onto her back. Her long hair splayed across the pillow, her green eyes looked like large uncut emeralds. "And you know the hard part now, there aren't a lot more surprises— not unless you've got a secret or two I don't know about."

"Please, God, no. I can't stand any more secrets or surprises. I just want everything normal." She looked up at him, eyes shimmering with tears. "Can't we just be normal, Lucio?"

"You never liked normal before."

Ana groaned and covered her face with her hands. "Maybe because I had no idea how abnormal I was! I'm scaring myself."

He laughed. He couldn't help it. She still had so much of the old Anabella in her. She sounded exactly like the fiery rebel he'd fallen in love with, the one that mocked rules, her family, and social convention.

He ran his finger over her warm cheek. "You are rather unusual, Anabella Cruz."

She gasped and caught his finger in her fist. "You called me Anabella Cruz. Are we still married, or was that just a slip?"

He hesitated. "A little of both," he finally admitted. "You did file for divorce, but it hasn't come through yet. But it should be final soon."

"So we are married."

"For about another week or two."

"But until then, we're still married."

She was impossible. He looked down at her and wondered how on earth they'd ever managed. Oh, the fireworks between them. The heat and sparks had been unreal. "Yes, we're married for two more weeks."

"Then let's renew our vows! Let's say them again and forget the divorce and stay husband and wife."

"Ana!"

"Why not?"

"You know why not. I've just told you why not. There are reasons you wanted out of our marriage and those reasons haven't changed. The problem is you can't remember those reasons but once you do—"

"I'll want to beg your forgiveness and ask you to keep me and we'll make this work, Lucio. We will. We can make this better than ever."

Lucio wasn't sure what to feel. Part of him was elated.

But another part of him was troubled. Ana's happiness was infectious but he knew she couldn't possibly make promises she wouldn't be able to keep. And once her memory returned...

"Let's at least give it a chance, Lucio. Please?" She gazed at him with such hope and trust that it wrenched his heart in two. "Don't say no. Not tonight. At least think about it."

How could he argue with that? "Okay. I'll think about it."

"Okay." She grinned and curled up next to him, her legs between his. It was the way they'd always slept. Connected. Tangled.

Ana slept but he couldn't. It was impossible to sleep when he was so aware of her body and his thoughts were circling madly about his head.

What she wanted was impossible. How could they start over? He didn't even know where they'd gone wrong! And if he did as she asked, if they did try again, when would she next tire of him?

No. He couldn't put himself through that kind of hurt again. He might love her. But he wasn't completely crazy.

But oh, it felt like heaven, lying here with her, feeling her warmth and sweetness surrounding him. Lightly, so as to not disturb her sleep, Lucio gathered Ana's long hair into a silky ponytail and held the mass in one fist.

Her memory was only just beginning to return and yet he'd never forgotten one detail of their life together.

He met her when he was twenty-seven and she seventeen, spotting her in La Boca, a colorful working-class neighborhood in Buenos Aires. She was haggling over a trinket at the open air Sunday market and he watched her go back and forth, getting the price lower and lower. He'd liked how her green eyes sparked and her cheeks glowed. Her lips were full and bare and yet even bare they looked like ripe berries, like the fruit that spilled profusely from the vines and shrubs to the fertile ground.

She'd been wearing a handkerchief knotted in her black hair. A long peasant skirt. Tight-knit short-sleeved shirt. She was as bohemian as they came and after five minutes haggling, when Anabella still couldn't afford the gold necklace, he bought it, and handed it to her.

She didn't thank him. She took the necklace and just stared at him, wide eyed, serious.

She didn't want to talk? She didn't have to talk. And inclining his head he walked away.

But she chased after him, falling into step beside him. "Where are you going?" she asked. Not who are you? Not, what is your name? Not, why did you buy me a necklace? But where are you going?

Lucio's chest warmed, remembering. Remembering his Anabella in the cute handkerchief and the straw sandals with the ties that laced halfway up her calf. Beautiful girl. Rebellious girl. She didn't want to be a Galván.

He didn't know she was a Galván until after the first time they made love. He knew nothing about her family until he'd tasted her skin, kissed every inch of her, made her part of him. Then when he knew, and when he realized who he'd taken, what he'd taken, not just Anabella's virginity, but her respectability, he knew he was damned.

They weren't the same. They'd never be the same. They'd never be accepted together.

Eyes heavy, sleep encroaching, Lucio pressed a tender kiss to Ana's nape. It had been an incredible adventure. This life, his life. He'd seen things he'd never thought he'd see. He'd done things a poor gaucho shouldn't have been able to do. And best of all, he'd loved Anabella.

Ana woke with a start, skin beaded with perspiration, heart thumping. Her hands flew out on either side to stop her fall. But opening her eyes, she realized she wasn't falling. She was lying on her back in bed. Next to Lucio.

She looked at him briefly, the sheet half covering his chest, one arm flung over his head in sleep. She saw the sinewy lines of his forearm, curve of bicep, thick deltoid muscle in his shoulder.

And looking at him she felt her heart twist.

She remembered everything he'd told her last night—and more.

She had been the one to divorce him. It had been her choice. She'd wanted to escape him, wanted to escape their life together.

Not because she didn't love him, but because she loved him too much and she felt too much and she couldn't bear the pain.

They'd had a baby together. They'd lost the baby—the baby of their heart—and losing that baby had hurt her body so much she'd never conceive again.

Ana swallowed around the lump in her throat.

Losing the baby was a huge issue for her, far bigger than she'd ever shared with Lucio. She didn't even know how much the miscarriage had upset her until someone offered her hope that the child—her and Lucio's child—still lived.

But it was all a hoax.

The hoax turned her life inside out. It had given her hope and made her realize how much she wanted the baby to exist. It had left her with nothing but a void.

She'd wanted the baby so much, she'd alienated Lucio.

Turning over on her side, she studied her husband who wouldn't be her husband much longer. With his arm over his head, the dense muscles in his chest and torso were stretched long and smooth. The silk coverlet rested low on his hips, the sheet hit higher.

He looked so beautiful and yet so remote. He'd been through so much because of her. She was grateful for his love, more grateful than he knew and she ached to close the distance between them. Longed for the intimacy they'd once shared.

Gently Ana pulled the crimson silk coverlet back, leaving just the soft cotton sheet over him. She could see the outline of his muscular body beneath the thin sheet. Legs, hips, ribs.

Her man, she thought, itching to touch him, press herself against him, feel his lovely golden skin against every inch of her. Lightly she touched his flat stomach and saw the muscles tense.

She remembered the intensity of being together, making love together, as if it were yesterday. She remembered the way she felt when she woke up in the morning after spending the night with him. She'd have such vivid dreams, such sensual dreams, dreams where she was certain he touched her all night.

Her heart beat faster. She wanted that again. She wanted that now and she felt almost weak with need.

She'd just give him a kiss through the sheet, a light kiss. That's all. She brushed her lips across his stomach. His abdomen rippled. She watched the taut muscles and then lightly kissed his hipbone.

Her mouth felt dry. Her heart was pounding. Scooting down on the bed Ana braced her weight on her elbows and leaned over his hips. Very, very lightly she touched the swell of his erection through the sheet, and as she exhaled, the hard shape of him grew harder still.

Ana felt a thrill. It was ridiculous but she felt the first little bit of control she'd felt in a long, long time.

Lowering her head she touched him again with her lips, leaving her mouth against him so he could feel the warmth of her mouth. He rose against her mouth and with the tip of her tongue she outlined the shape of his head, and his erection lifted even higher, pressing up against her mouth.

The thrust of his erection against her mouth made Ana's body warm. She craved his energy, knowing that every time they came together, it was explosive.

She wanted him now, wanted some of that fire now. Stroking him through the sheet had seemed like a good idea but now she was desperate for more. She wanted to feel as much as she could, she wanted to feel everything.

Need. Love. Desire.

Need. Love.

Need.

Ana sat up and slowly drew the sheet over his hips exposing his thick rigid length. She stared at him for a moment. She could do this, she told herself, just be careful.

Ana knelt over him and shivered as his warm body touched hers. Her thighs quivered and slowly, carefully, she lowered herself, his erection brushing the incredibly sensitive skin between her thighs.

She sucked in a breath, her body beginning to tremble. He'd been so adamant they not make love, but making love wasn't going to send her into seizures. She'd asked the nurse about sex and Patricia hadn't seemed overly concerned as long as she and Lucio took it easy.

They'd just take it easy.

They'd just take it long and slow.

And as she struggled with indecision she felt his erection against the inside of her thigh. His arousal was so hard, so hot, so smooth. She wanted him inside her. Holding her breath, closing her eyes, she slowly, very slowly lowered herself onto him, hesitating when she felt his thickness fill her, stretch her.

God, he felt amazing. He felt like everything beautiful and good in the world and with the air bottled in her lungs she pressed down, making herself relax to take more of him. She wanted more of him. She wanted all of him.

Exhaling slowly, she settled all the way down, feeling stretched and full and truthfully Ana was afraid to move. It had seemed like such a good idea but now that she was with him the sensations were so intense and the emotions so strong, she was almost overwhelmed.

And as she sat on him, torn by indecision, Lucio's hand clasped her bare bottom. "So *negrita,* what are you going to do now?"

She opened her eyes. His expression was sleepy, but definitely amused. *"Hola."*

He shook his head a little, his beautiful mouth curving.

"I've heard of a strong sex drive, but *chica*, this is a bit extreme, don't you think?"

Even as he said the words, he lifted his hips and thrust deeper into her. Ana gasped. His black eyebrows arched. "Like that, do you?"

And with another tilt of his hips he rocked her. He was barely moving and yet she felt him throb inside her and with each little action rubbed the base of his shaft against her tender lips and the incredibly sensitive nerves above.

The heat of him inside her, and the shape of him against her, was making her muscles tighten. She felt a ripple in her belly, a current that made her feel electric all over. "Stop," she breathed, leaning forward to press her hands against his chest. "I don't want to climax yet."

And he just grinned and rocked her again.

Damn, he was gorgeous, damn, he knew how to use his body, and damn, she was no longer the one in control.

He must have felt the tension building in her and his hands settled on her hips, fingers against her hipbones. He held her down, held her firmly against him, held her still and he was the only one moving as the muscles inside her continued to tighten, contracting slowly, rhythmically until they were squeezing helplessly around him.

"Stop," she choked, the pressure building, the intensity mindblowing.

"Not a chance."

And he just kept moving in her, deeply, insistently, rocking her world until her skin glowed hot and she felt as if fire lapped inside her, in her belly, and between her thighs. Ana groaned as he continued, pushing her further and further out into impossible sensation, to a place she felt only feverish tension, exquisite sensation and she dragged her nails over him, blindly, wildly, needing him to release her.

Still holding her, he rocked deep, thrusting up in her and she cried his name. The blue sky shattered in her mind, the blue pieces of the sky falling like diamonds. As the diamonds fell on them, coating them, making them sparkle,

Lucio's body surged within her, and this thrust was uninhibited, uncontrolled. He was with her, sharing the pleasure with her, and her body clenched his wave after wave, holding him tight as he shuddered inside her.

Ana fell forward onto his chest, exhausted, almost nerveless. *"Gracias, Senor,"* she whispered, weakly caressing his chest.

She felt him smile. *"Por nada,"* he answered huskily. You're welcome.

She relaxed on him, their bodies still joined. Comfortable, and finally at peace, she closed her eyes. She'd never loved Lucio as much as she loved him just then. "Remember our big plans?" she whispered huskily.

"Which ones were those?"

"It's not as if we had so many. Think." Her hand caressed his damp chest. "We had just a few dreams, but our favorite was running away together. Seeing the world together." She paused. "Seeing your world together."

"My world?" His voice was pitched low. He sounded close to sleep.

"Mmm. Your world. We've got two weeks before the divorce is final. Why don't we go do something exciting together? You know, kind of an end of a marriage honeymoon."

His hand stroked her hair. "Sounds a bit far-fetched, *chica.*"

"But no more far-fetched than a gaucho and aristocrat marrying."

His laughter was soft and it rumbled from his chest. "True."

"So what do you say?" she whispered, pressing a kiss to his chest. "You and me on one last grand adventure?"

"Está bien. Let's do it."

CHAPTER NINE

Lucio was gone when Anabella woke a couple hours later. The sun was high in the sky and the window was open letting the morning breeze in.

And there was no way that the next two weeks would be their last two weeks together. Yes, they'd have a grand adventure, but it wouldn't be a goodbye. Ana would never say goodbye. This adventure would be a chance for them to start fresh.

It was feasible. There was no reason her plan couldn't work. When it came to the two of them, anything was possible.

Maria stopped by the bedroom. "The Senor wants you to stay in bed and get some more rest," the housekeeper said. "Your breakfast is on the way."

Ana settled back against the pillow, not about to argue. She was grateful for an excuse to stay in bed a little longer and relive the incredible time she and Lucio had spent together earlier this morning.

It was nothing short of amazing. It had been so natural, so sexy and sensual.

And this wasn't going to be the end of their lovemaking, that's for certain! No, it was the beginning. It was the beginning of everything.

Even if Lucio didn't know it.

Lucio wanted to stay home with Anabella but if he and Ana were truly going to take off for a week on what she called "their last grand adventure," then he needed to get some things done at the winery office first.

In the morning he met with his team of managers at the

winery, and the afternoon was spent in Mendoza with industry representatives. They were still trying to hammer out an agreement with the California Wine Council and Lucio updated the Mendoza vintners on his Napa Valley meeting.

Returning to his vineyards later that afternoon, Lucio drove with the windows down, letting the crisp September sunshine fill his car.

He wanted Ana back. He wanted another chance to make their marriage work. He knew the odds were against him but he was a man who loved the long shot, a man who'd gained his fortune in a handful of reckless throws of the dice.

He'd earned a million dollars in one night.

He'd taken fifty thousand and doubled it. Taken a hundred and made it two hundred thousand. Taken two and made it four, and so on until he was gambling a half million dollars and calling himself foolish, calling himself brave, calling himself the last courageous man in the southern hemisphere.

He was a man who could lose everything and he'd long ago accepted that.

He could leave the casino with nothing but the shirt on his back, and he would still be all right.

He'd have no problem going home, back to the place where his people were poor but happy.

Being poor wasn't such a bad thing. There was a certain freedom in humble circumstances, and he liked living out of a knapsack, liked sleeping on the hard ground. With the wind in his face, the sun and rain in his eyes, he knew he was real.

Money, what was that? Houses and cars, who needed these things? All he wanted, all he ever asked for, was one true great love.

Lucio parked at the winery office, needing to drop off some files for his assistant before continuing home to the villa. But after parking, he sat in his car a moment, thoughts scattered, fingers drumming the steering wheel.

Just one true great love, he repeated, and Ana had been that love. But what now? What happened next?

Did he just say goodbye after their ''great adventure''? Did he let her back into his life knowing that at any moment she could reject him again?

He suppressed a sigh and left his car to climb the winery's low stone steps. His winery was one of the oldest in the valley, dating back over one hundred and twenty years. The stone building and cellars were original to the property, built in the 1880s as waves of new European immigrants settled in Mendoza, most of the immigrants from Italy and France. His land had been planted with the Malbec grapes from the Southeast of France and had later become the basis for Argentineans' beloved red.

The winery front door opened unexpectedly and Lucio nearly walked into Dante's solid chest.

If Lucio was surprised to see Dante, he didn't show it. ''Business in town?'' he asked Dante casually, leading the Count through the spacious reception to one of the smaller tasting cellars at the back.

''Yes.'' Dante bypassed a bar stool to sit on the edge of a massive oak barrel.

Lucio drew a bottle and two glasses from behind the counter. ''Anabella?'' Lucio guessed and was rewarded by Dante's wry smile.

Dante took the goblet Lucio handed him. He sniffed the red wine, gave it a slight swirl before he drank. ''It's good,'' he said taking a sip. ''Very good.''

Lucio leaned against the counter, breathing in the musty smell of fermenting grapes that seemed to permeate every stone in the old cellar. ''I like it, too,'' he said, thinking that even though he'd resisted this life here in Mendoza for the first couple years, he'd begun to settle into it, find it a good fit. As a vintner he was allowed to spend days close to the land, planting, testing, working the soil between his fingers, feeling the sun and rain on his back. It was a good life.

''Yours?'' Dante asked, taking another sip.

"Our new label."

Silence stretched. They avoided speaking for a few minutes, each taking measured sips from their simple balloon-shaped glasses.

It was a good life, Lucio silently repeated, forcing his tight muscles to relax. And Mendoza was his home now. With or without Anabella, he'd made this his place, and even if he wanted to go back to his world of the itinerant gaucho, he couldn't. He wouldn't know how.

Knowing this, he questioned how he could possibly go with Ana on this getaway. Did it make sense to make one last trip together? Was there any hope for them at all, or was he just continuing the fantasy?

And what was wrong with fantasy, a small voice taunted him. Ana *was* the fantasy. She'd been his fantasy from the very first day he saw her in the market square at La Boca.

It'd been a gamble from the start and he was still a gambler. He'd never been afraid to lose. If he couldn't take a risk now, what did any of it matter? What point was there in his success if he'd lost his courage?

If he went with Anabella for a week, what was the worst thing that could happen? He'd already lost his heart to her. What was left? His soul?

"How is she?" Dante broke the quiet. "How much of her memory has returned?"

Lucio felt Dante's tension. "Not as much as you'd like," he said, shifting his weight.

"Meaning?"

Lucio felt the weight of Ana's illness, the worry her family felt, his own fear that she might not recover. They'd all been through so much and until she was herself again, making informed decisions again, Lucio knew going away with her, playing a romantic role with her, was taking advantage of her. "She knows she's forgotten the past five years. She remembers that she's my wife."

Dante's brows lowered. "And the divorce?"

"I told her about the divorce, but she doesn't believe it."

Dante made a strangled sound. "Doesn't believe it? It was her idea!"

"Perhaps I should have said, she doesn't accept what I've told her. She still doesn't have all her memories back and because of the gaps in her memory, she still thinks of us as a couple."

"A couple."

He nodded. "She doesn't remember the bad things, Dante. Only the love."

Only the love.

Lucio felt the muscles along his back and neck tense. And a year ago she'd fallen out of love—something he'd never understood. How did one fall out of love? He'd never fallen in or out of love. He just loved. It was no easier, no more complicated than that. It just was. But Ana didn't remember the falling out of love, only the falling in love and she wanted another chance.

Another chance to break his heart.

Could he do it?

Could he not do it?

Dante was pacing the small cellar room. "She doesn't intend you both get back together, does she?"

Lucio's stomach burned as if he'd drunk acid instead of a wonderful red wine. He set his glass down, pushed it away from him.

He and Ana had never stood a chance, had they? Not when her family was so violently opposed to them.

And they were still opposed to them. But who the hell did they think they were? Throwing their weight against him? Against Ana? How could they possibly think their name, their wealth, their powerful connections meant more than his and Ana's happiness?

Lucio glanced out the narrow cellar window at the rolling hills. "You know Ana makes her own decisions."

"She *will* remember."

"I know." Lucio's head turned and his hard stark gaze met Dante's. He'd expected mockery in Dante's eyes but there was none. Instead Lucio saw...sympathy. But in some ways, the sympathy was worse than anger.

Dante reached into his pocket for his car keys. "I have something of Ana's. Didn't even know I had it. She left it at the hospital."

Lucio followed Dante out of the cellar, through the reception, back into the late afternoon sunshine.

Dante went to his car and retrieved a cardboard box. "There's not much here. Mainly papers and a couple photos, but Ana had insisted on taking it to the hospital with her so I imagine she'll want it back."

Lucio stared at the light blue box in Dante's hand. A shoe box. Pale blue with narrow white stripes. Ana's missing baby box.

So the box was real. Did that mean the baby...? He broke off, wouldn't let himself go there. There wasn't a baby, there never had been a baby. He couldn't even start to get his hopes up. "Do you want to come up to the house," he asked Dante, "give it to her yourself?"

Dante shook his head. "Not if her memory hasn't completely returned. I don't particularly like the bad guy role." He smiled grimly. "I never meant to be the bad guy."

"You're not."

Dante's smile faded and he ruffled his hair with a tired hand. "Just so you know, I wasn't part of Marquita's plan to bring Anabella home. I had no knowledge of it until I got a phone call saying Ana had a change of heart and was on her way to my house in Recoleta." He shot Lucio a swift glance. "I'm sorry."

Lucio shrugged. "As you said, it wasn't your doing."

"But you were hurt. Badly, I hear—"

"Water beneath the bridge." Lucio reached for the cardboard box. "What matters now is Ana's future, yes?"

Dante's expression looked grave. "Yes. Give her my love, would you? Let her know I'm thinking of her, and that Daisy and the children hope to see her soon."

Lucio drove up to the villa with the cardboard box on the

seat next to him. He shot several curious glances at the box, dying to know what was inside but unwilling to lift the lid. It was Ana's box. He'd give it to her. What she did next was up to her.

Anabella had spent much of the day going through all the closets and cupboards in the house. It was nearly five in the afternoon now and she sat on the floor of the study poring over nostalgic items she'd saved, examining old greeting cards, theater ticket stubs, airline tickets to far-away places and postcards she must have bought on trips and never sent.

She was still scanning the stack of postcards when Lucio entered the study. *"Hola,"* she greeted, looking up as he walked in. "I've been going through photos and souvenirs but I can't find anything from our wedding. Didn't we take pictures? I could have sworn we had pictures."

"They're at my apartment." He leaned against the door-frame watching her, one arm behind his back. "I was afraid you might dispose of them so I took them with me when I moved out."

He'd taken their wedding photos because he'd thought she'd throw them away. Wow. If that wasn't a statement about their relationship, she didn't know what was.

"I would have never thrown the pictures out," she said softly. "As confused as I was, as depressed as I was, I never stopped loving you."

"Why were you so depressed, Ana? What did I do?"

"You didn't do anything. It was me." She gathered a handful of papers and postcards and dropped them into the bottom drawer of her desk. She felt him watching her and she knew he was waiting for more, but how to explain to him that the whole baby thing had undone her? She'd gotten hopes up and when those hopes crashed she couldn't bounce back. Couldn't seem to find her feet—or the ground beneath her.

"But there wasn't any one thing?" he persisted. "You'd mentioned the baby before—"

"Yes, but it's not really logical, and if I try to explain you'll think I'm completely out of mind."

"Try me."

Ana shut the drawer and rose, brushing off the back of her brown linen trousers. She'd finally opened her closet doors and recognized her wardrobe. Odd how it was all slowly coming together, all the bits and pieces falling into place. Her life, her past, her emotions…they were finally beginning to make sense. "You really want to hear this?"

"More than anything."

She blew a black wisp of hair from her eyes and braced her hands on her hips. "You'll think I'm certifiably crazy, *flaco*."

His lips twisted in a small wry smile. "I already do, *flaca*."

She had to bite the inside of her lower lip to keep from smiling. He was undoubtedly the proudest, most stubborn man she'd ever met. And she adored that about him. "And if I do, you promise to still go away with me? You won't get angry and back out?"

"I won't back out."

She noticed he didn't say he wouldn't get angry. Well, at least he was honest. "Sit down." She took a seat on the study's small leather couch and patted the cushion beside her. "It's kind of a long, rambling story—"

She broke off, eyes widening as Lucio moved to sit next to her, the pale blue box on his lap.

"The baby box! Where did you find it?"

"Dante had it. Apparently you'd taken it with you to the hospital."

Hands shaking Ana took the box onto her lap and slowly lifted the lid. "Have you looked inside?"

"No. It's not my box."

Silently she lifted a thin blue airmail envelope from the box and opened the back, pulling out a rather grainy color photograph of a young boy.

Despite the blurry quality, it was easy to make out the

boy's dark hair, light-colored eyes, and pale olive complexion.

Lucio shot Ana a swift glance. "Who is this?" he said, taking the picture from her trembling fingers.

"Tomás. At least that's what Alonso said his name was."

"Who's Alonso?"

"Alonso Huntsman. The man who contacted me."

Lucio heard what she was saying but couldn't tear his gaze from the photograph of the young boy. The child, probably part European and part Indian, looked desperately poor. His black shorts were too big for his narrow hips and his faded T-shirt too small. He was barefoot and his dark hair had been cut short, the front quite unevenly. "Cute kid," he said, voice rough.

"I know. And for one week I thought he was our son." She leaned forward, pointed to the photograph. "He has light eyes, a bluish-green color. His age seemed right."

His age seemed right for what? Lucio looked at Anabella. Did she really imagine this could have been her son...*their* son?

Ana, carida. You miscarried.

The words were there foremost in his mind. They were there dangling on the tip of his tongue. "Explain this to me," he said gently, wanting to understand. "What made you really believe the child could be yours—especially since you know you miscarried at six months?"

"Because I didn't miscarry in my sixth month." Nervously she looked up, touched her tongue to her lower lip. "It was my eighth month and I went into premature labor." She could barely look at him. "You know me, Lucio. I'm not very good at confronting bad things. I'm better at ignoring problems than facing them—"

"You *miscarried.*"

"No. I went into labor and I delivered the baby."

"You never told me."

"Because *you* weren't *there.*" Her hands clenched and she gazed up at him with tears of pain and outrage shimmering in her eyes. "I was alone in that godforsaken boarding school. Age eighteen and giving birth—the pain was unbearable."

Her pale jaw worked. "I *know* there was a baby. I could have sworn I heard a cry. But then later when I asked to hold him, I was told he'd died." Her shoulders twisted. "I wanted to hold him. I needed to hold him—just hello—" she paused "or goodbye—but I'd lost a lot of blood and I was rushed to the hospital for an emergency transfusion."

"Why weren't you at the hospital?"

"Because I delivered the baby at the school. A midwife came. It was the normal procedure. Many girls had babies there."

"Did most babies die?" Lucio retorted bitterly.

"I don't know. The girls still expecting and the new mothers were kept in different sections of the school."

His brow grew darker. "I bet."

"They said it was because new mothers have different needs, and there was a nursery—"

"Did you see the nursery? Were there babies in it?"

She suddenly shivered. "Some," she whispered. "A few."

He wanted to shake her, demand why she hadn't told him this before, but he couldn't bring himself to speak much less touch her. It was all so incredible. Too impossible.

"Maybe the baby was stillborn." Ana swallowed hard. "But I never had a chance to say goodbye. I never saw him at all. And without that closure…"

That he understood. "And Tomás?" Lucio prompted, realizing for the first time just how much Ana had kept buried inside her, realizing that she'd never really grieved, nor shared her sorrow with him.

Ana stood, suddenly restless. "Last year, about this time, I had a phone call from the man I mentioned, Alonso Huntsman. He asked a lot of questions about where I went to school, and if I'd ever been pregnant."

"But why would he even call you? What business was it of his?"

"He said he had an old relationship with the Galváns and felt an obligation to look into the rumors he'd heard about a Galván baby for sale."

Lucio inhaled. "A baby for sale?"

"On the black market." She pressed her hands to the back of one winged chair. "I heard nothing from him for a few days and then the photo arrived."

"Tomás."

She nodded. "I didn't know what to think. It was surreal—the child in the photo was about the right age and yes, he could have been mine, but then, he could have been anyone's. There are many mixed race babies here, and all Argentinean children are beautiful."

"Senor Huntsman called me a few days later—remember, Lucio, this happened in less than a week—and apologized for getting my hopes up. He was quite nice, but firm. He said that after further investigation the little boy couldn't possibly have been mine. Tomás was about a year too young."

"And that was the end of that?"

"More or less."

He picked up the photograph again and stared down into the child's face. "What if he *had* been ours?"

Her lower lip quivered. "I don't let myself play that game anymore. We don't have a child. Whatever I hoped for, whatever I wished for, will never be."

Lucio set the photo back into the box. "I wish you'd told me. I wish I'd known. I would have wanted to do something for the child, even if he wasn't ours."

Ana suddenly covered her face. *"Don't."*

"I was just saying—"

"I know what you were saying. You would have tried to help the child, tried to do something good for the child. Don't you think I've thought that a hundred times since then?" She looked up, face pale, expression stricken. "I didn't tell you on purpose, Lucio. I was being mean. Selfish. I didn't tell you because I didn't want you helping him!''

His eyes narrowed. ''I don't understand.''

''Yes, you do. You know me well enough to know I'm not a saintly person. I'm selfish and petty...'' Her voice faded away and tears spilled. ''And I hate myself for abandoning him. I wanted to help him and I didn't just to spite you.''

''Anabella.''

She pressed a fist to her mouth, so icy on the inside, feeling like a glacier slowly melting. ''I've been mad at you for ages, Lucio. I didn't realize how angry I was until I couldn't—wouldn't—help a four year old child.''

His expression was one of utter disbelief. ''Why were you angry?''

She was so ashamed she couldn't even answer him, couldn't put into words such deep, unreasonable rage.

''Ana.''

Wiping her eyes, she drew a deep breath. ''I—I blamed you.''

''For what?''

She shuddered. ''The miscarriage.''

Lucio took a swift step back, muscles tight, coiled. He couldn't believe she'd just said that. He took another step away. ''I was as devastated by the loss as you, Anabella.''

''If you hadn't left me in the square—''

''I didn't leave you! I was *dragged* away.''

''I know that with my head, but in my heart I wanted you to rescue me. I wanted you to save me from that awful girls' school I was sent to in Uruguay.''

His eyes burned. His chest felt as if it were on fire. ''I didn't know where you were, Ana.'' He didn't add that he couldn't walk for months after the beating, or that her mother's henchmen had done such a thorough job they'd broken nearly every bone in his legs.

She said nothing and he swallowed the bitterness of the

past, the sour taste in his mouth making his stomach turn. "Why have you waited so long to tell me this?"

"I remember being terrified that something terrible would happen to Tomás if we didn't find him. I couldn't stop thinking about him. Couldn't stop worrying about him. I knew if you came home you'd help me. I knew if anyone could save Tomás, it'd be you."

"Oh, Ana, I can't believe what you're telling me. I can't believe this is why you divorced me."

She gripped the chair tightly. "I didn't want the divorce—"

"Didn't want the divorce?" He spun around to face her. "Don't kid yourself, *carida*. You were so angry with me, so full of rage and resentment, you stopped talking to me. You refused to make love with me. You asked me to move out of our bedroom into the guest room. Ana, that was all *you*."

She knotted her hands, practically pleading. "But I didn't really want to be without you. I just didn't know how to stop what I had started."

He swore softly. "Ana, you're killing me."

"It's true. I mean it. I was scared to death by what I started, scared by what I was feeling. Yes, I was angry, but I realized as time went on, it wasn't really at you. I was angry at life, angry with everything and everyone—"

"I can't do this." He held up a hand. "It's been a hard week, Anabella. It's been a long week. Your illness has put us all through a lot."

"Forgive me, Lucio."

"It's not that easy."

She swallowed and lifted her chin. "Fine. I'm not asking for an easy way out. I'm just asking you to give me a chance—"

"*A* chance? I've given you dozens!"

Tears glittered in her eyes but she lifted her chin even higher. "So what's one more?"

CHAPTER TEN

LUCIO'S mood didn't improve in the four hours between Ana's confession and dinner. In fact, by the time Maria called them to the table, he was seething.

During the meal he virtually ignored her, and once Maria cleared their plates, Lucio pushed back from the table and walked out.

Ana watched him leave, heart aching. Oh, she'd made such a mess of everything. She hadn't explained things very well in the study and yet even if she had a second chance, she wasn't sure she could explain it any better the second time through.

Suppressing a sigh, Ana left the dining room and headed in search of Lucio. She found him in the study on the telephone. He didn't even look at her when she opened the door.

Ana stood there, waiting, until he finished his call.

"What now?" The look he shot her was pure contempt.

Her stomach knotted. She would have walked out if it weren't for Tomás's little face haunting her. He was so young to have too-weary-for-this-world eyes. "Will you help me find him, Lucio?"

Lucio rocked forward in his chair. "So you can do what? Send him an annual Christmas card?"

"No. I have to know how he is. I have to know he has a good home—"

"I can pretty much guarantee you he doesn't."

She flinched. "Then maybe we can help him."

"Did you think to ask your Senor Huntsman for more information?"

"I haven't been able to find Alonso. The phone number

he gave me is no longer in service. It's been out of service for nearly eleven months now.''

"So you did try to reach Huntsman?''

"Yes. I spent weeks trying to hunt him down. I even hired a private investigator—without any success.''

Lucio's dark eyes met hers and held, his black eyebrows savage slashes, his nose long, a little thick through the bridge, a hint of his Indian ancestors. "Is this when you started pulling away from me?''

"I'm sorry.''

"Okay.'' His jaw flexed as he battled to hang on to his temper. "I've things to do,'' he said, nodding at the door. "We'll talk more in the morning.''

He stared at the closed door for long minutes after Anabella had left.

He didn't know what to think. Or feel. Anabella was clearly worried about the little boy and yet she'd been against adoption their entire marriage. What did she want with Tomás? Did she even have a plan?

Lucio sat up half the night working on his computer, sending out e-mail enquiries to every government agency, every adoption agency, child welfare group he found listed. In each e-mail he asked about Alonso Huntsman and mentioned that he was looking for a young boy approximately four or five years old, with dark hair, blue-green eyes, and probably living in a poor orphanage outside the Buenos Aires province.

He went to bed late, and as he slid beneath the covers, Ana sleepily moved into his arms. For a long moment he just held her, his head bent to breathe in her sweetness and warmth. Her long hair brushed his arm and her slender frame curved against him. As his heart ached, suffused with wave after wave of intense emotion. She felt so right in his arms. She had from the first moment he held her and even now, more than five years after they met, he knew he was made for her. Made to love her. Protect her.

He'd never want anyone else like this.

Ana stirred in his arms, and lifted her face to his. "Kiss me," she whispered, wrapping an arm around his neck and pressing closer, the crush of her soft full breasts a torment and a pleasure.

"It won't end with just a kiss," he warned, stroking the length of her, savoring the curve of her waist and hip.

"It better not."

They made love with an almost quiet desperation and fell asleep tangled together. Lucio woke first, saw it was still dark outside, still quite early, and carefully left Ana so he could return to his desk.

Lucio made himself a cup of espresso in the dark cavernous kitchen, carried the small steaming cup to the study and turned on his computer hoping someone had responded to his inquiries. But nothing positive came in.

He began his search anew, sending out fresh queries, researching related names, refusing to give up on his lack of progress or leads.

Taking his breakfast at his desk, he reached for the phone at nine and dialed Dante's office number. "Good morning," he greeted Dante. "I'm sorry to bother you at work."

"Anything wrong with Anabella?"

"No. Not exactly." He and Dante were still not close, still not overly friendly but at least they were no longer at each other's throats. Perhaps progress had been made. "Dante, I need some information about Ana's boarding school in Uruguay. Did you ever speak to the doctor who treated her?"

"No. Why?"

"Do you know for certain that Ana miscarried?"

There was a long pause. "I spoke with the headmistress of Ana's school," Dante answered, his tone incredulous. "She called me from the hospital saying that Ana had miscarried and needed emergency medical treatment."

"There was never any mention of a baby?"

"No. What is this about?"

"Anabella was approached a year ago by a man named Alonso Huntsman—"

"Never heard of him."

Lucio had thought as much. He felt his temper rise. Had someone deliberately tried to blackmail Ana? Had there been a plan to pass Tomás off as her son? Or had someone really thought that the boy could have been Anabella's? "But you don't know for certain that she miscarried? It's possible she could have delivered a healthy baby."

"She *didn't*."

"You weren't with her, Dante. You sent her away for a period of months."

"To *school*."

A school for unwed, pregnant teenage girls, Lucio thought. A school that specialized in very quiet adoptions.

"She finally graduated, matriculated," Dante continued. "She passed her exams."

Lucio felt a rise of irritation. Dante was being particularly obtuse. One could pass an exam and still give birth to a baby. And Anabella was intelligent. She could handle tremendous pressure if sufficiently motivated.

A moment of strained silence stretched across the phone line before Dante spoke again. "You don't really believe there's a child, do you?"

No. Yes. Lucio dragged his teeth over each other. It depends if you wanted to call Tomás her son. "There's a child we're interested in. I'm sure Ana will tell you more if we can locate him."

Lucio spent the rest of the day down at the winery office. He had his assistant on the phone, while he continued researching on the computer. He was determined to find someone, somewhere who might know something. But at the end of the day he'd come up with nothing and he felt even more frustrated than he had the night before.

It was dusk when he returned to the villa. The house was relatively quiet and then he heard laughter coming from the kitchen. Lucio wandered into the kitchen and found

Anabella sitting on a high stool at the island with a toddler on her lap. She was bouncing the baby and playing patty-cake and it was rather enchanting, Ana and the baby, and Ana's green eyes warm with love.

"Senor!" Maria cried. "Look who's here! This is my grandbaby, Jorge. He is coming to stay with me this weekend. Isn't he lovely?"

"He really is," Ana murmured, pressing a kiss to the baby's chubby cheek. "He's very good. He likes everybody. Do you want to hold him, Lucio? He won't cry."

"That's all right. Jorge seems to like you," he answered, lightly touching the toddler's small hand.

Jorge smiled and gurgled and grabbed for Lucio's finger. Lucio smiled, some of the gloom he'd been feeling all day lifting.

"Is he getting heavy?" the housekeeper asked.

"Not at all," Ana answered, gazing down into the little boy's beautiful face. "He's gorgeous. You're very lucky, Maria."

"I know." Maria clapped her hands and reached for the baby. "I better go take him back to his mama or I'll never get any work done."

Lucio noticed that there was nothing simmering on the stove and just a few vegetables chopped on the cutting board. "Don't worry about cooking for us tonight, Maria. You have your family here. Go enjoy them. I think I'll take Anabella out to dinner tonight. We haven't been out for a meal since I returned home."

It wasn't until he and Ana were at the staircase that he thought to actually ask her if she wanted to go to Mendoza for dinner. "I'm sorry. I didn't even ask you. Would you like to go out?"

She didn't even need to speak. He could see the happy shimmer in her eyes. When Ana was happy, the world was happy.

An hour later they were seated at a small French bistro in downtown Mendoza. The restaurant had the best chef in the city and there was usually a wait but the restaurant featured premium wines from Lucio's vineyard and the maître d' quickly found a table for them at the window.

Ana looked radiant in a simple long gold lace dress with thin gold satin straps. The dress hugged her slim figure and with her long hair loose, Lucio couldn't take his eyes off her.

God, she was beautiful. No one moved like her. No one smiled like her. No one had such a throaty, sexy laugh. In the candlelight she literally glowed.

Just like their wedding day.

"It's been quite an adventure with you," he said, thinking he was lucky to have known her, lucky to have loved her despite the problems of the past year.

He saw a flicker of fear in her eyes. "I hope it's not over yet. You did say we'd have one last crazy fling."

"Actually, I don't remember it being a crazy fling. I thought we were just going to do something. Go on one last vacation to the beach, or Buenos Aires."

"Or Patagonia to the Perito Moreno Glacier."

The place they were married. "And why would we go there?"

She grinned, her green eyes glowing like emeralds. "To renew our vows, of course."

Lucio laughed once. "Now I know you're out of your mind."

Ana heard his sarcasm but she felt warm on the inside. She loved how Lucio was looking at her, loved his half-amused, half-exasperated laugh. And best of all, she loved remembering their wedding.

It'd been so exciting getting married in Patagonia, above the glacier. It'd been rather raw and wild, saying their vows in the south of Argentina, in the middle of a sea of white ice. She'd believed they were marrying in Nature's church. She told herself that the penguins in their little tuxedos were the choir, and the seals, whales and black-necked swans the congregation.

"You were a beautiful bride, Ana," he said, voice quiet. "I have regrets, but marrying you isn't one of them."

"What do you regret then?"

"Spending so many years trying to get you pregnant. Making love only because you were ovulating." His jaw hardened. "I think all the energy we put into making a baby would have been better spent focusing on us."

"Probably."

His mouth curved. "I can't believe you actually agree with me on that."

"It's taken me a long time to accept that I'll never conceive again, but I understand that now. I'm okay with it now. I'm honestly ready to move on."

But before he could answer, his wireless phone rang. Lucio glanced at his phone. "I have to take this call," he said, pushing his chair back even as the waiter arrived with their dinner plates. "Don't wait for me, Ana. Go ahead, eat. I'll be back in a moment."

But he wasn't back in a moment. He was gone nearly twenty minutes.

"I'm sorry I missed dinner," he said, when he reappeared. "But it was an important call."

The whole time Lucio was gone Ana thought about the events of the past two days. She knew she'd made a mess out of things yesterday, and she hadn't conveyed what she'd wanted to share most—that she wanted Tomás. She knew the child wasn't biologically hers but she no longer cared. She felt responsible for him, and she needed to know he was really okay.

"Do you want a coffee?" Lucio asked, seeing that she'd finished.

"No. I'm quite content. Thank you."

"Let's go home then." And Lucio signaled for the dinner bill.

He was upset about something, Ana thought as Lucio paid the bill. He was trying to keep up a good front, but there was something eating at him, something in the phone call must have set him off...

Ana glanced at him as they left the restaurant. "What was the phone call about?" she asked, drawing her matching lace wrap closer, trying to sound casual.

They crossed the street and Lucio unlocked the car door. "I might have to go away for a couple days. There are some things I need to do."

"Where are you going?"

"North. To Salta."

Salta was his home.

She slid into the passenger seat. Lucio shut the door after she was safely in. She waited for him to climb behind the wheel. "Can I go with you?"

"No."

"Why not?"

He didn't feel like arguing. He shook his head and started the engine and pulled away from the curb.

It was Alonso Huntsman who'd called tonight. Alonso Huntsman who'd interrupted their quiet dinner. Huntsman had heard through an unnamed source that Lucio was looking for him and he'd called Lucio to make it easy for him.

Alonso had agreed to meet Lucio three days from now in Salta, in front of the cathedral. Lucio couldn't help wondering if Huntsman knew that Salta was his home. Huntsman seemed to know quite a few things and it made Lucio uneasy.

"Please, Lucio." She was still pleading her case.

"No!" He couldn't do this, he was out of patience. "This is a trip I have to make alone."

Anabella changed in her room, stripping the gold lace dress off and putting on her nightgown. Dinner had started out so promising but it'd ended like everything else—a disaster.

What was wrong with her and Lucio? Why couldn't they make this work?

She stood at her window and looked out to the distant

mountains. The mountains were so dark it was difficult to distinguish them from the night sky.

She heard a sound below and leaning forward on the windowsill, she spotted Lucio outside on the veranda.

So he was still up.

Ana slipped a silk robe over her gown and went downstairs to join him.

As she stepped outside she saw he'd lit the cigarette but wasn't really smoking. He was just staring at the glowing red tip, watching the cigarette burn to ash.

Lucio heard her approach. He turned his head. "Why wouldn't you ever consider adoption?"

His question surprised her. She crossed her arms over her chest. "Because we were trying so hard to make a baby of our own."

She watched his face, knowing full well that the issue of adoption had once been a bone of contention between them. Lucio had wanted to adopt. She hadn't. But at the time she and Lucio had the argument, she was still grieving her own inability to conceive. It had been impossible to think of adopting at that point. She'd still been so determined to have a child of her womb, a child to replace the one she'd miscarried several years earlier.

"But I don't feel that way anymore," she added softly. "If we could find Tomás…"

"And if we can't?"

She hadn't thought of that. "I guess we could explore adoption."

Lucio glanced down at the tip of his glowing cigarette. "You mean, *if* we'd stayed together."

She felt her stomach plummet. "But we *will* stay together."

"I can't say that. I don't think it's true."

"You're just tired. The phone call has upset you."

"Yes, I am tired, but that's not the issue. You know, Ana, I wish I'd been there when you were eighteen. I wish I'd been able to rescue you from that school, save you from losing our baby. But I wasn't.'' He suddenly crushed out his cigarette. ''And you *did* lose the baby, and you *were* hurt. Quite frankly, Ana, I think there's too much that's gone wrong between us, too many mistakes—''

''No.'' She'd been listening to him in appalled silence but she couldn't listen to this any more. ''I'm not going to let you walk away. You can't just walk away. We've been through so much.''

''Too much.''

''If you love someone, there's never a point it's too much. If you love someone—''

''Spare me the crappy greeting card sentiments. I don't buy them. Neither do you.''

She wanted to push him down into the patio chair. Wanted to press him backward and crawl on him, sit on his lap facing him, facing them, facing the truth that she knew he loved her. She knew he'd always love her. It was so basic. Their need and attraction had been there from the beginning like the wind and the rain. It was elemental, basic. It'd been there forever and it'd always remain.

Maybe he couldn't stop loving her. But that didn't mean he couldn't try. And the trying would kill her.

''I won't let you do this,'' she said quietly, fiercely, filled with fresh resolve. ''I will find a way to make us work.''

He tossed the cigarette butt into a ceramic ashtray on the glass topped table. ''I said the same thing not even a year ago. I fought it, too, and you didn't care. You wanted no part of a second chance, or reconciliation.''

''Well, I was wrong.''

He laughed, short, sharp, angry. ''God, Ana, you are something. You make me crazy. You make me even doubt myself.''

''Good.'' She went to him then, and saw how he took a swift step backwards. Every step forward there was a counter move. They were in an endless game of chess. And he'd block her moves every chance he could. He might be

King but she was Queen and in chess the Queen could beat a King. Easily.

All she had to do was keep her focus, and not lose nerve. She wouldn't lose nerve. She wouldn't lose period.

"I want you to doubt yourself, *flaco*." Her eyes met his and she saw his brows lower and his features tense. "I want you to be so full of doubt that you can't leave me, can't walk out the door without giving us one more chance. Without giving us one more real chance to work this out."

"That's not going to happen."

"How can you be so sure?"

He smiled grimly. "Because I know me, and I know you. You're fighting for us now, but you're not fighting out of love. You're fighting because you're scared."

She couldn't even answer that. She sucked in a breath and stared at him, eyes burning.

He must have seen how he'd hurt her as his expression gentled a fraction, his eyes warming. "You talk tough, *carida*, but underneath all the fire is a sheltered and inexperienced woman. You're not afraid of losing me. You're afraid of facing life on your own."

Ana's nerves felt stretched and her head buzzed with sound. In her head she heard his voice, heard her own protest but it all blurred together.

She walked to the edge of the veranda, facing the garden with the softly splashing fountain. "Maybe I am relatively inexperienced, and maybe I have been sheltered. I was raised differently than you. You've been able to be whoever you want, travel wherever you want—"

"I wouldn't call riding a horse around the pampas traveling," Lucio interrupted dryly. "And it seems to me you've done exactly as you pleased."

She knew he wasn't talking about lifestyle, but her attitude. He was referring to her rebellious disregard of her family's wishes.

"For all your desire to be different," he continued, "you're the most mercurial woman I've ever met. You say one thing and yet you do another. You claim to want this and yet you choose that. You like the idea of being simple, but really, you can't live without all this.''

His dark head inclined, indicating the romantic villa drenched with moonlight, the elegant mysterious gardens with the musical splash from marble fountains. ''You were made for this life, *negrita*. You cannot live without this...without these.'' His lips curled and he was coolly mocking, almost amused. ''You are these things.''

Ana had gone cold when he started speaking but by the time he finished she felt hot, flushed with anger, her cheeks burning. ''You know nothing about me!''

His lashes lowered. ''I know too much about you.''

She stood still, on the edge of the veranda, feeling as if she were teetering on the brink of disaster. And yet she was frozen, incapable of taking a step in any direction.

The silence stretched between them so awkward and uncomfortable that Anabella felt tears thicken the back of her throat. He didn't like her. He didn't like who she was or what she represented.

She hated the silence. She hated the intense emotions he aroused in her. He made her feel as if their whole relationship was a farce, as if their relationship had been based only on physical attraction. But were they just about skin...chemistry...sex?

Ana looked past Lucio to the pretty villa's plaster walls and high narrow windows framed with light green shutters. She could see the wall of climbing vines and hear the fountain's gurgle, the water splashing against the marble's slick surface.

No. Lucio wasn't right. Their relationship wasn't based on sex. It was real, their emotions, their needs, their dreams. This was real. And this—beautiful or ugly—was love.

She balled her hands into fists, trying to hide her fear. ''It's easy for you to criticize me, because you know my life. You know my past. But I don't have that advantage. I know next to nothing about your home, your family, your world. I know only that you spent much of your life free and that you gave up that freedom to marry me, and I wish I could see what you've seen, wish I could know a little of what you've known.''

"It's not a life for women.''

"Your mother—''

"She is part Indian. She is from the mountains.''

And in his voice she heard the unspoken, *but you are not.*

"Maybe I'm not from the mountains,'' she said, her voice thickening, "but I'm no weakling. I can ride a horse. I can cook over an open fire. I can camp out—''

"Our life isn't camping.''

"You're going to make this difficult, aren't you?''

He laughed, low, impatient. "You're the one that likes a good challenge. Everything's got to be difficult. Demanding. Intense.''

Her cheeks burned with a flood of heat. He was far angrier than she'd imagined. And it crossed her mind that she might have already lost him. It might already be too late for him.

But she wouldn't accept that. She couldn't lose him.

She wouldn't lose him.

"You've always been a gambler, Lucio. So take a last gamble on me. Take me with you when you go home in two days. Let me see where you grew up, where you lived, where you went to school. I want to know you better, and I very much want to meet your family.''

Her eyes searched his and in his dark eyes she saw heat and fire and a smoky desire that took her breath away. But he was going to contain the desire, control the desire, maybe even lock it away.

"It would mean a lot to me,'' she added gently, trying somehow to express her love, trying to find a tender spot somewhere in his angry, battered heart. "I know your father passed away this year, but I'd still like to meet your mother. Your brother. Your cousins…the friends you grew up with.''

"Very few are left in my village. There'd be almost no one to see."

"But the village—"

"Is small, poor, uninteresting."

"Can't I make that judgment for myself?"

"It's not easy to get there, and you've been very ill."

"You know I'm better. Call Dr. Dominguez. He'll clear me for travel."

Lucio didn't say anything and she felt as if she was fighting a losing battle. "I'm not asking for the moon, Lucio! I just want to be with you. I want to get to know the gaucho side of you. Besides, it'd be fun to see new places, try new things."

"Then book a cruise. They're pretty ships and they travel to safe ports. No danger. No harm. No problems."

"You're being cruel."

"I'm being honest."

She was nearly out of arguments. There wasn't much more she could say. And then she knew she had one last plea, the one that was the cheap shot, the desperate shot, the one she hated to use but she'd use it. It was the ultimate power play. "If you love me, Lucio. If you ever loved me—"

"Ana." His voice was harsh, low, warning.

She saw his jaw pull, the muscles working silently, but she ignored the warning. This was important. They were important. She had to somehow find a way to repair the damage between them and perhaps if she could go to the place he'd been raised, looked into his world, she could maybe connect with him in a new way. A better way.

"If you loved me," she repeated, "you'd do this for me."

Slowly his lashes lifted and he stared at her with unwavering intensity, eyes so dark she could see nothing but her own reflection there. "You want to go?" His deep voice bit at her, weary, caustic. "Okay, you'll go. We'll leave tomorrow."

CHAPTER ELEVEN

Lucio saw Ana's eyes light. "When tomorrow?" she asked, excitedly, sounding impossibly girlish.

He'd already planned to leave in the morning, and while taking Ana hadn't been part of the plan, maybe it was better this way. Maybe it was time everyone stopped tiptoeing around Ana; stopped shielding her from unpleasant things; demanded that she finally grow up and accept responsibility for her own needs and emotions.

"What time should I be ready?" she asked in a breathless rush.

His gaze held hers, trying to intimidate. "Early."

She wasn't the least bit troubled. She merely blushed a little and drew her robe closer to her chest. "Good. I can't wait."

"Neither can I," he drawled, wanting to be irritated by her enthusiasm but this was what he'd always loved about her. "You'll need to pack tonight. Take only as much as you can fit into a knapsack, and get some sleep. We'll leave before the break of day."

In her room, Ana packed lightly. She pressed a pair of jeans, shorts, long cotton skirt, one decent blouse, a couple of T-shirts, sandals, and a fleece lined weatherproof jacket into the small bag. She'd wear boots and another pair of jeans and after adding clean underwear and a nightshirt into the knapsack, she'd run out of room.

Lying in bed Ana couldn't help the rise of hope. No matter what Lucio said, this was an opportunity to start fresh, make new memories, be wild and free like they'd once been together.

She just had to be positive. Had to keep a good attitude.

No matter what Lucio did or said, she'd make this fun. She really would.

The knock on her door hours later seemed to come in the middle of the night. Ana heard the knock sound again, the rap even harder, shorter, sharper, and eyes barely open, she peered at the clock. Three-thirty. *Three-thirty?* Good God, the man had to be kidding.

Dragging herself into a sitting position, she told herself he was just kidding. Tormenting her a little. There was no way he really intended to set off at three-thirty in the morning.

Ana shoved a long wave of hair from her face and staggered to the door. Opening the door she discovered the hallway was dark. The house was dark. She could barely make out Lucio standing tall and ominous in the hall.

"You're pulling my leg," she croaked, rubbing her eyes. He knew she hated waking early, knew that he knew she was a total grouch before seven a.m.

"You're not ready?"

His deep voice was low, taunting. She could barely make out his face in the dark but she had the distinct feeling he was smiling. "Now I know you're kidding."

"Time to go."

She leaned against the door and smothered a yawn. "We're leaving now? At three-thirty in the morning?"

"No. We're leaving at three-forty. That should give you ten minutes to get some clothes on and meet me at the stables. And *negrita,* listen carefully. If you're even one minute late, I'm going without you. I'm not going to wait."

He was serious. She heard the hardness in his voice, the absence of all tenderness, all affection. "Lucio," she whispered his name.

"Don't push it, not now. Not today." His dark eyes looked black in the dim hallway. "I feel like I've spent my whole life waiting for you and I'm done. I'm tired. We'll go on this trip and then I'll bring you home, and when I bring you home, I'm gone."

"Gone?" she repeated softly, heart stopping, dropping, falling like a bird killed in flight.

"*Sí, Senora.*" His teeth flashed for a moment, white and then the smile disappeared. "I'm moving on."

Stomach knotted, Lucio headed downstairs, into the kitchen where he picked up the saddlebags he'd packed with food. He'd been unnecessarily rough with Anabella and he didn't like it.

Yes, he was upset, yes, he felt hurt, but what was the point in taking his anger out on her? Where was the justice in making her suffer just because he felt like hell?

None of this was her fault. She hadn't gotten pregnant without his assistance. She hadn't wanted the miscarriage, hadn't contacted Alonso Huntsman, hadn't sent for the picture of the boy. Huntsman had come to her. Huntsman had stirred her imagination, given her hope. He couldn't blame Anabella for not coming to him. She'd been bitterly disappointed. He understood her disappointment. He felt strangely the same way.

Lucio's long strides carried him out of the house and out towards the stable. The night air was still quite cool. Anabella would need a jacket. By noon though, the weather would be warm, and the sun in the mountains fairly hot. He hoped she knew to dress in layers. She ought to know. But he'd check with her before they left just in case.

Anabella appeared in the stable dressed in jeans, T-shirt, a red poncho-style sweatshirt and boots. Her long hair had been loosely braided and with her red wool poncho, he thought she could have passed for a *china,* a gaucho's woman.

He found the corners of his mouth lifting. Except for the proud tilt to her nose, no one would have known she was Count Galván's youngest daughter.

"All set?" he asked, taking her travel satchel from her. He'd already saddled her mare and he rolled her bag inside a blanket and tied it onto the back of the horse.

Ana approached her horse curiously. "This isn't my saddle,'' she said, lightly touching the leather *correon* which had neither pommel, horn, or cantle.

He glanced up. "It's the gaucho's saddle. If you're going to go home with me, you go home like me."

Years ago she'd seen the way he saddled his horse and she'd found it quite complicated. However now as she watched his strong hands lift and adjust, she found the layering of leather squares and woollen pads fascinating.

As she watched him she remembered the waterproof *sudadera* always went on first against the hide, followed by the *matra,* a rough woolen blanket. The *carona* went on top of the *matra,* and that was a supple piece of cowhide to brace the *bastos,* which were two stiff bars of leather forming the saddle frame. Finally, the soft leather *correon* and thick sheepskin fleece rested on top.

"Let's see how the stirrups fit you," he said, circling her waist with his hands and lifting her into the comfortable saddle.

She felt the warmth of his hands despite her sturdy denims. One of his hands brushed her bottom as she settled into the thick sheepskin. "Careful, *flaco,*" she warned. "I'll sit on that hand.''

Lucio shook his head, his black hair scraped back in a tight ponytail, his thick black lashes hiding his expression. "Is that supposed to scare me?"

"Maybe a little." She made a face at him. "Now that you know I'm so difficult to control."

"You're difficult, but not difficult to control," he answered, smiling faintly. "You aren't so different from your temperamental horse, and *chica,* I've *never* had a problem with your horse."

She grinned despite herself, amused by his perspective. Lucio had raised her horse from a foal. He'd given the mare to her as a wedding gift and she'd later learned that he'd trained the mare himself as well as introduced the feisty mare to a saddle.

Now Lucio was extending her leg, checking the placement of her boot in the stirrup. "Feel okay?" he asked, his hand briefly running up her shin before touching the back of her calf.

He was touching her lightly, touching her through her boot and yet she felt shivers race through her. Her belly did a flip and her body felt hot all over. She wanted him badly, wanted his hand beneath her shirt, against her breast, wanted to feel his hard body pressed to hers, hip to hip, chest to breast. She wanted so much and it seemed like forever since they'd spent a full day in bed doing nothing but touching, kissing, making love.

"Is this okay?" he repeated.

She clenched her teeth, feeling her sensitivity grow. "Depends what you're asking me to feel."

Lucio caught her dark braid and twisted it around his hand, drawing her head down close to his. "You're awfully brave this morning, *negrita*."

She saw his dark eyes blaze and the heat scorched her. He was still the hot-blooded cowboy that melted her heart. She longed to bend lower, press her mouth to his. She longed for a taste of him, one long slow kiss followed by the brush of his tongue.

"Don't know why," she answered huskily, unable to keep the emotion and need from her voice. "I didn't get half enough sleep last night."

"Should have gone to bed earlier then."

His voice was cool, almost detached but his cool voice contrasted with the fire in his eyes. He might think he could control his desire for her but he couldn't hide it. He couldn't keep something that strong a secret.

"Should have let me sleep in," she answered, tugging against his hand, trying to free herself from his hold. "You know what I'm like on less than seven hours sleep."

His fingers buried tighter in her hair. His lips curved ever so slightly. It crossed her mind that he still loved the tug-of-war between them. Loved the tension and resistance.

Anabella knew that no woman had ever given Lucio such a run for his money before.

"I remember when you used to get by on four hours," he said, drawing her head down, closer to his face, inches from his lips. "I remember when I'd make love to every inch of your body and you never slept then. You were too hungry. Too alive."

She couldn't breathe. Blood surged to her face and her lower belly throbbed, aching for him. He was making her feel hot. Sensual. Wicked.

She'd been his. She'd always be his. He'd loved her so intensely, so completely, he'd practically branded his name on her. There was no way she could ever love another man, no way she could ever sleep with another man. Lucio was her answer. Lucio was her other half.

But there were problems between them now, more problems than they'd ever had and it'd take time to work through everything. Time and patience.

And more than a little bit of humor. "But that was then," she answered sweetly, breathlessly. "You were so much younger then. I doubt you'd be able to…sustain…such pleasure now."

She saw his dark eyes spark. She'd pricked his considerable male ego. "You don't need to worry about my stamina, *negrita*. I am stronger, even more controlled now. I can hold back, hold on, as long as I'd like." His eyes glinted danger. "As long as you'd like."

Oh. Her eyes opened wide and she felt heat prickle across her skin, high on her cheekbones and along her full bare mouth.

She felt his gaze slowly travel across her burning face and then settle on her lower lip which was throbbing now. *Just kiss me,* she silently pleaded. *Just kiss me, Lucio. Now.*

"But you won't know, will you?" he concluded almost sadly, sliding his fingers from her hair and giving her thigh a firm pat before stepping away from her. "Because you wanted out. You were tired of me. So be glad, Anabella, you got what you wanted. You're practically free of me.''

"I'm not free yet," she flashed back, boots pressed down into the stirrups, rising higher in her sheepskin seat. "And *flaco,* neither are you."

He shot her a caustic glance and lifted his broad brimmed felt hat from the hook on the wall. "Close enough," he retorted, dropping his hat on his head and swinging himself up into his fleece even as he took the horse's reins in hand.

Ana tried not to crave him as he settled into the stirrups, his long legs even harder, more muscular now than when Ana had first met him. Five years of civilization hadn't hurt him, she thought. It had added solid muscle to his large frame, and a sexy sophistication that barely hid his raw sensuality.

His raw sexuality.

The night they'd first made love, the night he'd taken her virginity, his hands had been everywhere, his mouth everywhere, he'd explored her as if she were his to own.

And she had been.

But now he was riding away from the stable into the still dark night and Ana, despite being all roiled up on the inside, her emotions churning, her body hot with wanting, had no choice but to follow him.

She'd asked for an adventure and he was going to give her an adventure. But maybe, she thought, riding hard to catch up with Lucio, maybe the adventure would also help her find her way home to him.

It had been a long time since Anabella spent more than a half hour in the saddle and by noon her thighs ached. By three o'clock she was ready to call it a day.

"How much further?" she asked as they paused in a streambed slicing through the high red rocks to give the horses a chance to drink. She'd been prepared to be saddle sore. She hadn't prepared herself for the heat. Even though it was early spring, the sun seemed unnaturally intense in the rocky terrain.

Lucio leaned forward on his stallion. "Had enough of my life already?"

She wiped a bead of moisture from her brow. Lucio had taken his hat from his head and plopped it on her own hours ago. "You need it more than I do," he'd said and she'd wanted to protest but couldn't. The sun's brightness was almost too much for her and she kept forgetting she didn't have the strength she'd had from before her illness.

"No," she answered, mustering a tough-girl smile.

But Lucio's dark eyes narrowed as they scanned her face. His mouth tightened and his expression turned grim. "Your head hurts, doesn't it?"

"It's nothing, Lucio."

But the tightness at his mouth didn't ease. He swore softly. "This is too much for you. It's too soon after your infection."

"Lucio." She leaned forward, touched her hand to his thigh. "I'm fine. I want to go on. *Please.*"

His gaze held hers another moment and then he reluctantly nodded. "*Está bien.* Let's go."

They continued to follow the dark blue river through the canyon floor, beneath the odd canopy of trees. The trees grew in clusters and they'd ride sometimes twenty minutes before reaching another shady grove.

It was nearly dusk when Lucio dismounted at one cool green grove. "We'll stay here tonight." He walked to her side and taking her by the waist, lifted her down. "Let's unsaddle the horses so they can wander a bit and graze."

She glanced around them. There were no fences, no boundaries in site. "You won't tether the horses?"

His eyebrows lifted. "Why? They won't go anywhere. They know better. Unlike you, they respect me."

Flushing, Ana concentrated on unsaddling her mare, lifting each layer until the horse was completely free. Running her hand across the mare's warm hide, Ana was pleased by her mare's condition. "There's no bruising at all," she said.

"Of course not. A gaucho that abuses a horse is no gaucho at all.'' He drew a towel from one of his saddlebags and began to rub his stallion down. "There are only three things sacred to the gaucho, chica. His horse—which is his freedom. His *facón,*" Lucio said, touching the knife he wore tucked in the back of his belt, "which is his protector and companion."

"And the third?" she asked.

"His *china,* his woman."

For dinner they ate meat, cheese and onion empanandas Maria had made the day before, and even though the small flaky pastries weren't fresh out of the oven, Ana couldn't remember anything ever being so tasty. "Where are we now? Roughly speaking?"

"Not quite five miles outside of San Juan."

San Juan was just a short jaunt from Mendoza by car. "We're still a day's ride from La Rioja," she said numbly, beginning to realize the number of days they'd be in the saddle. Days and days and days.

"Doesn't feel like we made much progress, does it?"

"I thought we'd gone farther."

Creases fanned from his eyes. "It's not so exciting being a gaucho."

"I'm having a great time," she lied, hating the way her eyes burned, tears of exhaustion not far off. She stretched out on her bedroll so Lucio wouldn't notice. "This is fun."

"*Sí,* Senora. It's an adventure."

She closed her eyes, trying to ignore his mocking tone. He was going to love making her miserable.

Suddenly she felt something hit her arm. Ana opened her eyes and saw a chocolate bar lying next to her on the blanket.

"Dessert," he said. "Enjoy."

And she did. She lay on her blanket, and stared up at the sky and took small bites, savoring each one. She'd forgotten how silky smooth chocolate could be and how dark chocolate melted even more slowly than milk chocolate. There was something exotic and sensual about it, and yet there was comfort in it, too.

When she was little her father used to take her for a stroll with him through their Belgrano neighborhood in Buenos Aires after Mass on Sundays. They had one of the biggest houses in Belgrano—took up nearly an entire city block—and the Sunday walk was something for just Papa and Anabella.

Her father knew everyone—or maybe it was everyone knew her father—and he'd stop in at different shops, have a coffee at the café, buy a newspaper, visit with the different pretty girls in stores before buying Ana a treat at the corner store on their way home again.

And every Sunday, week after week, month after month, year after year, he would hold the door for her as if she were a lady and very gravely wait for her to select her sweet. And every Sunday, she'd pick the same thing—a bar of Swiss chocolate wrapped in gold foil. Each Sunday she'd offer her father one of the little squares and each Sunday he smilingly, politely refused.

It was their private little ceremony, and she had no idea how much she'd treasured their Sunday ritual until her father died. Surprised by the poignancy of the memory, Ana turned on her side. "My father could be very loving," she said softly.

"No one's all bad," Lucio answered, from where he lay against his bedroll. Then suddenly he reached for her hand, caught it in his and pressed a kiss to the inside of her palm. "Not even you."

He'd made her smile. She nodded, and lay back, heart aching a little. "Thanks, *flaco*."

"No problem, *flaca*. Good night."

It seemed like minutes later he was shaking her awake. "Open your eyes, sleepyhead. Time to go."

Ana's eyes fluttered open and staring up, she saw the wispy blue sky overhead and blinked. "Already?"

"We have a long ride before we stop for breakfast. We better get going. I've an appointment in Famatina I can't miss."

After a couple hours of riding they left the rugged red rocks behind and dropped down into the Famatina Valley with its smattering of cactus and near desert-like conditions. Once on the valley floor, Lucio loosened his reigns and let his stallion go. It was all Ana could do to stay close.

It was midmorning by the time they reached Famatina and Lucio led them through some back streets until he stopped at a very simple corner café. While tethering the horses to a nearby tree, he asked Ana to order them some coffee and pastries.

They sat with their espressos outside. During their breakfast Lucio glanced at his watch a couple times. "Just who are we waiting for?" she asked, feeling Lucio's growing tension.

Lucio drained his espresso. "Alonso Huntsman."

Ana choked on her coffee. She nearly slammed the cup in the saucer. "Alonso Huntsman?" she repeated.

He nodded and his gaze skimmed the relatively quiet street, one side and then the other.

"He's going to meet us here?" she persisted, incredulous.

"That's what he said."

They continued to wait and now Ana had butterflies in her stomach. Lucio drew out a small knife and began whittling away at a piece of wood. She watched him whittling, the silver blade glinting in the sun. "You are such a gaucho."

He looked up, eyebrow cocking. "*Gracias*, Senora."

Suddenly a car parked next to the café and a young woman in a beige suit stepped out. She glanced at the café, and then at the cluster of tables on the sidewalk. Her expression cleared as she spotted Lucio.

She approached their table briskly, extending a hand. "Senor Cruz?"

Lucio stood but he was suddenly wary. "Yes?"

"Unfortunately something came up in Mr. Huntsman's schedule," the young woman said in crisp Spanish, clearly the Spanish learned in schools and college instead of as a native tongue. "He has sent me here in his place. He asked me to give you this."

She smiled apologetically as she held out an envelope to him. "Good luck," she said with another brisk smile. "I'm sure Mr. Huntsman will eventually be in touch."

The woman returned to her car and drove away and as her blue car disappeared down the road Lucio opened the envelope.

He studied the top sheet of paper. "At least we know Huntsman isn't a criminal," Lucio said, turning the paper around so Anabella could see it. "Instead your Alonso Huntsman is a British intelligence agent."

Ana reached for the paper. "A *what?*"

Lucio began to laugh with relief. "A spy."

CHAPTER TWELVE

"A spy?" Anabella repeated, eyes lighting. She'd always loved mysteries, drama, great adventure stories. "You mean, like James Bond?"

"Well, I can't imagine he's as glamorous as 007, but yes, he works for the government," Lucio answered, sorting through more of the papers in the envelope.

It was actually quite a thick bundle and a page beneath Alonso's note was a list of names, addresses, and phone numbers. It appeared to be a contact list Alonso had put together, people who'd had contact with Tomás or once had been part of the boy's life.

"They're all leads to Tomás," Ana said, running her finger over the addresses clustered in the Northwest provinces—La Rioja, Catamarca, Salta, Jujuy. "We're not far from where he's been living."

"Or was living," Lucio corrected, excitement fading as he read Alonso's notations in the margins. "These are dead leads. Apparently the child has disappeared from the orphanage."

"Disappeared?"

"Alonso says he's gone. Can't find a trace of him."

He felt Ana stiffen. "That's not possible," she protested. "The orphanage must have records. They must have documented his coming and going. Someone removed Tomás from their care. Surely they didn't allow a child to leave without recording who collected him. Children just don't vanish into thin air!"

Not unless something bad has happened, Lucio thought grimly. But he didn't share his fears, concentrating instead on sorting through the mountain of paperwork in the envelope. There was so much here, so much more than he'd originally thought. Copies of records, a birth certificate that had obviously been dummied, photo copies of a journal.

Ana peered over his shoulder, trying to see what he was reading. "And just where is the orphanage?"

"Outside San Salvador de Jujuy."

"Oh, Lucio, that's not far. It's only a couple of hours drive from Salta." She grabbed his arm. "Let's go. Let's get a car and drive there today. We could be in San Salvador de Jujuy by late this afternoon."

Lucio didn't answer, too engrossed in the notes Alonso had written. Alonso indicated that the orphanage, although claiming to be a charitable organization, didn't appear to be legally operated. Children, Alonso noted, appeared and disappeared with alarming regularity. Even the staff had a high turnover. There'd been four different directors in the past year alone.

He turned the page, looking for more information on the orphanage, *Casa de Niños,* which lay tucked high in the mountains of San Salvador de Jujuy. From what he gathered, *Casa de Niños* was a small facility, sheltering approximately twenty children, mostly Indian children—descendants of the Incas. Yet if a small facility responsible for only twenty children didn't remember Tomás, had no record of Tomás, something was very amiss.

Anabella squeezed his arm. "Come on, Lucio. Let's get a car. We're wasting time. We could be in San Salvador de Jujuy before dinner—"

"Not so fast, Ana. We've got the horses. We have a huge number of dead ends—"

"Maybe they're not dead ends!" She gripped his arm tightly. "Maybe Alonso didn't know what to look for. Maybe he didn't ask the right questions. San Salvador de Jujuy is high in the mountains, remote from the rest of the world, and Alonso is foreign. It makes sense that people wouldn't trust him, that they'd be reluctant to talk to him.

But you're part Indian. The people would trust you. They'd talk to you. I know they would.''

She was so passionate right now, so determined to find Tomás, especially since the child seemed to have vanished into thin air. But they both knew children didn't just vanish. Something had happened. The question was, what?

The Northern provinces were bordered by Chile and Bolivia and five years ago a band of outlaws wandered back and forth over the Andes, preying on small towns, extorting businessmen, kidnapping members from the wealthier families, demanding ridiculous ransoms. A shocking number of babies and young children disappeared, rumored to have been sold to wealthy families overseas under the guise of private adoption. Then two years ago the ringleaders had been rounded up and locked away. Almost immediately the kidnappings stopped, the business owners no longer harassed, and life had returned to normal.

Or had it?

Lucio drew a slow breath. Ana had called Alonso Huntsman a foreigner but Alonso was more than that. He was a secret agent. He worked for the British government. How had he learned about Tomás? How did it come to his attention that the child was being passed off as a Galván? What *was* Alonso Huntsman doing in the area?

It crossed Lucio's mind that perhaps there was far more here than one missing boy.

Black market. Child for sale. Ana's earlier words rang ominously in his head.

Maybe young children were still being trafficked in the region, but now, more secretly.

Maybe Alonso was more involved in the case than he was willing to admit.

Maybe Alonso knew where Tomás was—maybe he knew what had happened to him—but couldn't, or wouldn't share the knowledge yet.

Lucio needed to speak to Alonso. Something in the information in the envelope—including the lack of information—made him suspicious.

"So you're saying we're not going to do anything?" Ana planted herself before Lucio, forcing him to meet her gaze. "We're just going to sit around and wait?"

He glanced down at her. Her lovely face looked so expressive, so beautiful, and so perfectly furious. She'd always be passionate about people and life.

"We're going to proceed slowly," he answered, not wanting to disappoint her but his protective instinct was strong. There was no way he'd jeopardize Anabella's safety. He'd have to do some investigating on his own before he exposed her to any danger.

"And just what does that mean?"

Her green eyes sparkled dangerously. Her temper was up. She was fighting mad now.

He bit the inside of his cheek to keep from smiling. Angry Anabella he could handle. He knew how to fight fire with fire. "I'm going to make some enquiries before we head north," he answered calmly. "I want to ask some questions…narrow the scope of the search."

She shook her head, muttering something unflattering about arrogant macho men beneath her breath. "So that's it? We go back to the villa and I sit around while you make phone calls?"

"We're not going back to the villa, and I'm not making any phone calls. We'll continue as we've been, riding north, stopping here and there. I have friends along the way."

She shook her head again, her cheeks a dusty red. She was battling to keep control, battling not to say something she'd later regret. "But I don't want to keep riding. I can't play this gaucho game anymore. I want to get a car, go to Jujuy. I want to visit the orphanage, talk to the director—"

"Who has been replaced," he interrupted gently. "*Casa de Niños* has had four different directors at the orphanage in the past twelve months." A fact he'd discovered in Alonso's notes and setting off new alarm bells in his head.

Why would an orphanage go through so many directors? Who was supporting the orphanage? Who was hiring and replacing the directors?

The orphanage might be a cover for illegal activity. And yes, Lucio very much wanted to visit such a place, but no, he'd never take Ana there.

"Ana, you said you wanted to know my world. You said you wanted to know my family, my people. Well, I'm going to show you, if you let me—"

"But Tomás—"

"Is missing. You yourself said Alonso couldn't find the child because Huntsman is Anglo. So let my people, the people who live here in the North, help us. They can, Ana. But our ways aren't the telephone and the chauffeured limousine. We won't learn anything new by barreling into town. We'll just make people suspicious."

She looked away, her eyes watering. "You really think your people can help?"

"If we let them. But you must be patient. You must realize, *carida, you* are now the stranger, the outsider. As we continue north, you'll meet people who mistrust you as much as your family mistrusted me."

She closed her eyes and a single tear slipped free. Lucio's chest felt tight and he reached out and wiped the cool tear from her flushed cheek.

"It will not be easy for you, Ana, because you like things your way. You like to be in control, but this time, in this instance, we must do it my way. Can you do that? For us?" He hesitated. "For me?"

Her jaw worked. She swallowed with difficulty and then her thick black lashes slowly fluttered open. Her eyes were liquid with tears but they met his directly. "Yes."

Satisfied, he slid the paperwork back into the envelope and tucked it inside his leather belt and then steered her into a small shop where he bought sandwiches, cookies and bottles of water. He packed their lunch in his saddlebags and then they left town, heading back towards the mountains to climb the foothills again.

Back in the saddles, they rode hard for the next several hours, crossing one small stream and then another before climbing back into the hills which were the pale green of early spring but would bleach to gold and brown before long.

But the passing scenery was little more than a blur to Anabella, her thoughts centered solely on the mystery surrounding Tomás.

Who had taken him from the orphanage? According to the information collected by Lucio, someone had removed Tomás from *Casa de Niños* between September—when she'd first been contacted last year—and December, when Tomás's name didn't appear on the list of children receiving small Christmas gifts.

But maybe it was a good thing he was no longer at the orphanage, she told herself. Perhaps they'd found Tomás a loving family. Maybe they'd even found his real parents.

Deep down Ana knew she was kidding herself. A child that poor, a child that age, wasn't going to have parents magically materialize after all these years.

Hot and irritable, Ana pulled her poncho off, over her head and tied it around her waist. She was hot. And damp. And sick of riding a horse. She wanted a car. She wanted a highway. She wanted answers now.

But Lucio had said she had to trust him. He'd said they needed to do this his way.

Anabella suppressed a groan, hating relinquishing control almost as much as she hated the idea of spending another three or four days in the saddle.

She was not, she'd quickly realized, a *china*.

As if sensing Ana's mood, Lucio wheeled his stallion around, his narrowed gaze taking in her hot flushed face, and irritable scowl.

"We're not far now," he said encouragingly. "Stay with me, *negrita*."

She mopped at her brow. "I'm trying."

"I know it's a hard climb, but the effort will be well worth it."

It was all she could do to keep from crying. In Buenos Aires it was easy to forget the sheer size of Argentina, but out here, in the most northern part of the country, the landscape stretched from daunting mountains to endless salt plains, tropical forest to misty hillsides.

He knew what she was thinking, too, and his dark eyes flickered with warmth. "Not enjoying yourself, *flaca?*"

Ana mustered a taut smile, feeling as prickly on the inside as she did on the outside. "No, Senor. Your woman is enjoying herself very much. *Gracias.*"

He threw back his head and laughed.

An hour of steady climbing resulted in reaching another mountain pass, followed by a descent into another deep red and coral ravine with a shimmer of blue at the bottom.

"Is that smoke?" she asked.

"My friends. We'll camp there tonight."

There were about seven gauchos gathered in a makeshift camp at the edge of a small lake, all dressed in simple pants, loose white shirts. Some had wide leather chaps tied over their pants, and others wore leather vests and woven blankets folded over one shoulder.

By the time Lucio dismounted, one of the gauchos was already boiling water, preparing *maté*, the traditional Argentine tea.

Lucio was enthusiastically greeted. His back was slapped, his hand shook. He was hugged by nearly all of them.

Then conversation stopped and all heads turned, the focus now on her.

Lucio introduced her with disconcerting casualness. "Anabella," he said. *"Mi mujer."*

My wife. My woman. And just that quickly, the gauchos lost interest in her, returning their attention to Lucio and the horses. The horses were unsaddled. The bags and bedrolls tossed beneath the shade of an old gnarled tree. Then Lucio and the men stretched out around the fire to smoke their hand-rolled cigarettes and drink *maté*.

Ana sat on her own for nearly an hour, growing increasingly restive as the men talked and laughed. She couldn't believe how fast Lucio forgot about her, and leaning against the rock, she tried not to fume as the *maté* gourd was passed round and round and all the men took turns draining the gourd before refilling it. The *maté* ceremony could last for hours and this one looked as if might go on all night.

Worse, did any of them invite her to join? No. Did Lucio offer to include her? No. He truly had forgotten she even existed.

Finally Lucio stood, brushed the red dust from his trousers and approached her. She saw his boots in her line of vision but didn't look up.

"Do you want to bathe?" he asked.

And still she didn't look up. She didn't belong here. These others didn't want her here. She sensed that right now not even Lucio wanted her here.

"There's a hot thermal pool behind the boulders," he continued evenly. "It's quite protected and no one will bother you. You'll have complete privacy."

"I don't have a towel," she said huskily, unwilling to tell him just how insecure she felt at the moment. She wasn't prepared for life like this. Didn't know how to sit around a campfire or bathe naked in lakes and streams.

"I do."

He unpacked a towel and she found some clean clothes. Ana followed Lucio away from the campsite, past one of the massive rocks and they entered a small steamy clearing.

It was exactly what he'd said. A lovely private thermal spring. She bent over and touched the water with her fingers. The temperature was perfect. "Are there many thermal baths like this?" she asked, standing.

Lucio tugged on the elastic band confining her braid. "A couple in the area, and a great many more further north near Fiambalá."

"It's due to Ojos del Salado," he added, combing through her braid, untangling the thick black strands.

The volcano.

She shivered a little as his fingers touched her neck, her back. It was so easy to give herself over to him. She was so tired and his hands were so steady and strong. She loved his confidence, especially when he touched her. There had never been anything tentative between them.

Ana turned to face him, her long hair tumbling down her back. "Will you come in with me?" she asked, feeling an almost physical need to be close to him, part of him. They'd only been here with the others an hour and already she felt like such an outsider. This was a man's world. A gaucho's world. She felt as if she'd stepped onto an alien planet.

"I can't, *negrita*. I need to rejoin the others. It's important I sit with them awhile—"

"But you have!" She pressed herself against his chest. "You've been with them for an hour."

"You know *maté* can take hours."

"But why can't I join you?"

"Because you're going to take a bath."

His tone might be quiet, reasonable, but she knew he wasn't asking her. He was telling her and Ana felt hot tears start to her eyes.

He stroked her cheek with the pad of his thumb. "There's no need to be upset. We're just catching up on news and you know I want to ask about Jujuy, and *Casa de Niños*. One of the men here, Victor, is from that area. Another is from Humahuaca. These people know the north, Ana. That's why we're here. To get information, to ask some questions, to see if they can't help us in our search."

"But I want to be part of this. I want to be included."

"It's different here, Ana. Gauchos often live apart from their women for long periods of time. Gauchos—and gauchas, too—are very independent and men and women don't mix all day, all the time."

She ground her teeth together, feeling ridiculously childish. She knew his people had their own customs, their own culture, but it stung, being excluded. *Now she knew what Lucio felt like when surrounded by her family.*

He caressed her cheek again. "I can't ask for their help, *chica,* if you're sitting with us."

She nodded, slowly absorbing that she was getting a taste of what Lucio had lived all these years in Mendoza.

He returned to the others and she slowly stripped out of her dusty, sweaty clothes. Anabella soaked in the hot spring until her muscles were warm and liquid and her skin threatened to shrivel up. After drying, she dressed in the long clean gauze skirt she'd brought and a soft cotton top and returned to the fire.

For one brief moment she felt a half dozen different pairs of eyes on her and then all returned to their various tasks and conversations. Silently she moved to the bedrolls that Lucio had spread beneath the massive gnarled algarrobo tree and sat down. The fire was smoky and her hair was drying rapidly.

Lucio returned to Ana's side. "Miss your blow-dryer?" he asked, watching her try to comb through her hair with just her fingers.

There was a hint of laughter in his voice and she looked up at him. He had also recently bathed. His skin gleamed gold. His wet black hair was pulled into a sleek knot and he looked sexier than ever. "No. I like letting my hair dry naturally. It's better for my hair."

His dark eyes mocked her, contradicted her. He knew she'd never had to rough it before, knew that despite her rebellious streak she was accustomed to luxury. Five-star hotels. Catered dinners. Housekeeper, laundress, chauffeur. "Glad to hear you enjoy the out-of-doors. Now it's time to eat a true gaucho dinner."

She feared the worst when Lucio said "gaucho dinner," but the *mbaipoi* served, a porridge of cornmeal and meat, wasn't half bad. After dinner, the simple dishes were rinsed and put away, and the large stew pot overturned and left to dry.

The men settled into small groups by the fire. Ana drew her poncho on and returned to her seat on her bedroll beneath the tree. Some men played cards. Others talked. Another produced a well-worn guitar.

Lucio chose to lounge with the men around the fire. Ana gritted her teeth and told herself it didn't matter. He was a man. These were his friends. Remember, she told herself, he doesn't get to see them often.

And he does love you, she whispered to herself, fighting the loneliness with truth. No matter what happened between them, he would always love her, just as she would always love him.

For a while the guitarist played on his own, but after a half hour one of the gauchos turned the stew pot over and began to drum on it.

The guitar played the central melody and the drummer improvised. The tempo was fast, strong, with a bright clear rhythm, and to Ana, the melody sounded like sunshine at night—warm, vivid, intense.

After a moment Lucio left the others and moved to her side, nudging her thigh with his knee. "Scoot over."

She did and he sat down next to her, an arm sliding around her. Silently they listened to the music and eventually one of the gauchos, the oldest of the group, got up to dance. The others clapped as the grizzled gaucho danced, his hands lifted, his feet doing a series of swift intricate steps almost like that of the tango.

There was a huge history to the tango, Anabella remembered. The word was of African origin, and a blend of the *habenera,* brought to Latin America by Cuban seamen, the *payadas,* improvisational songs of the gauchos, and the *candombes,* the pulsing rhythm of the slaves.

In Buenos Aires the different cultures came together and the music styles met and evolved. Men were the first to dance the tango and watching the old proud gaucho dance now, Ana realized that she'd never really known Argentina, not the way she was beginning to know it now.

Music echoed off the rocks and the clear night sky.

"Don't be angry with them," Lucio said after a moment, speaking softly so no one would overhear. "They don't dislike you, Ana. They just don't know you yet."

"I understand." And she did. The gauchos' mistrust of her was no different than her family's mistrust of Lucio and she knew how hard it had been for Lucio, those first few years together.

It was probably still hard for Lucio but he didn't complain. He didn't object. He just learned to adapt.

"I know they just want what's best for you," she added, slipping her hand into his.

He bent his head, kissed her cheek, near the corner of her mouth. "You are the best." His dark eyes shone at her, a bit wicked, a bit playful. "*Really* the best."

Sparks shot up from the fire, sizzling into the dark sky. The pop of the fire was followed by a second shooting stream of sparks. The sizzle of red into the night reminded Ana of a volcano erupting.

Like her and Lucio. Hot. Passionate. Molten. She curled her fingers into his, craving him all over again. "Can't we go somewhere?" she whispered. "Be alone somewhere?"

His lashes lowered, concealing his expression. "You can't live without sex, can you?"

She felt a stab of intense emotion. "It's not sex I can't live without, Lucio. It's *you.*"

His lashes lifted and she saw the fire in his eyes, felt the intensity and knew he craved her as much as she did him.

He rose, and with her hand in his, tugged her to her feet. "Come on. We have things to do."

They traveled far from the others, past the first secret thermal bath to a small sheltered area further away. Entering the clearing, Lucio walked her backwards until she bumped up against a rock and inhaled sharply as his body brushed hers.

It'd been days since they'd last been together and she was dying to be close to him again, dying to have her bare breasts pressed to his chest, his hand on the curve of her hip, his body hard against hers.

Slowly, and with great concentration, she slipped her fingertips across the upper planes of his damp chest, her fingers sliding beneath the fabric of his shirt, feeling the smooth satin of skin over taut muscle, feeling the silky pebble of his nipple. He was dragging in a deep breath, one after another, and she felt him shudder as she circled his small hard nipple with a damp finger.

"You don't want to do that," he muttered hoarsely.

She felt a thrill of pleasure, a pleasure edged by danger, a pleasure that was so unique to the two of them. He knew her. She knew him. And they loved to push themselves to the brink. "Yes, I do."

"No woman touches me like that and gets to walk away."

She hid her smile by leaning forward and touching her mouth to the V of skin left exposed by his open shirt. She brushed her mouth to his skin, opened her mouth a little so he could feel the warmth of her mouth and the cool caress of her tongue.

His hand reached up to bury itself in her long loose hair. She closed her eyes as his fingers tangled in her hair, holding her head still against him.

He might be able to hold her still, she thought, but he couldn't capture her tongue. And she flicked the tip of her tongue across the hollow of his hard chest, between the thick planes of muscle and was gratified to feel his fingers twist deeper into her hair, and feel him press her even closer to his strong body.

He wanted her.

He wanted so much with her.

He wanted so much from her.

She slipped her hands up the backs of his thighs, felt his

muscles tense and she flicked another tongue kiss against his chest. "You know what I want."

"You're not exactly subtle."

She grinned, her smile hidden by her bent head. "Was I supposed to be?"

"*Negrita,* you play with fire."

He sounded so hoarse, his hunger barely controlled.

She lightly kneaded his small firm backside. "I love fire."

And suddenly his hand was beneath her skirt, his fingers sliding beneath the scrap of her silk thong. "Then you shall have fire," he mouthed against her ear, his tongue swiping across the sensitive outer shell, "and more."

She loved the play of his hand against the curve of her backside, loved his total disregard for underwear, for preliminaries, for things other men would think were so essential. He wanted her and his touch was hot with possession.

"Promises, promises," she answered, teasingly.

Lucio reached for the hem of her blouse and stripped it over her head. She hadn't been wearing a bra and without her blouse she was already half naked.

He growled deep in his throat, his hands covering her breasts, cupping her breasts and he pressed her backwards until she was leaning against the rock, completely immobile.

"It was no empty promise, nor an empty threat," he whispered against her ear before catching her wrists in his and lifting her hands over her head so she couldn't escape. He adjusted his grip, taking her slender wrists in one hand, leaving the other free.

With her rendered captive, Lucio's head descended and his mouth touched the full curve of her breast. She felt the rasp of his beard against the sensitive skin and the cool flick of his tongue across her taut nipple. She moaned softly as he covered the aching nipple with his lips. He sucked her, lavishing attention with his mouth, his tongue, even his teeth. He was waking everything within her, stirring every nerve, every memory of pleasure.

She squirmed helplessly as he lifted his head and settled on the other breast, but this time he just circled the areola with his tongue, wetting her, bathing her, and she felt so hungry for him, so hot for him, she could barely stay on her feet.

"Don't move," he said, freeing her hands, letting her arms fall to her sides. "You're mine now. You belong to me."

Crouching down, Lucio unbuttoned the side buttons on her long gauze skirt, and watched intently as the thin fabric fell to her feet. With his eyes he feasted on her, taking in the paleness of her skin, the flatness of her stomach, the shape of her body from thigh to hip.

Leaning forward he pressed a kiss to the inside of her thigh, and then another kiss a little higher on the same thigh.

The air caught in her throat as he slid her silky thong down over her hips, pushing the scrap of fabric to her feet. He pressed her even further back against the rock, exposing her to him.

She felt so naked and so vulnerable and yet it was incredibly sensual, too, knowing that she did belong to him, heart, mind, body and soul.

Lucio touched his mouth to the apex of her thighs, finding her warmth. He kissed her intimately, his mouth touching her gently, possessively, using tenderness to melt her. There was no way she could resist this, no way she wanted to resist this. With his hands and mouth on her, she felt her desire blaze hotter, brighter, sweeping any inhibition away.

He could do what he wanted to her and she knew she'd enjoy it. He could eat her alive and she'd just beg for more.

Her hands settled on his head as her body began to tremble. His tongue was so delicate, his patience endless, and he was drawing the pleasure out, refusing to let the incredible sensation peak too quickly. She shuddered as tension coiled hot and hard inside her belly, shuddered again at each flick of his tongue. Her fingers tangled in his dark crisp hair. She held him tightly, afraid her legs couldn't hold her.

"It's too much," she choked, skin flushed, body burning.

His husky laugh echoed softly in the starlit night. "It's never too much for you."

CHAPTER THIRTEEN

WITH his hands and mouth he aroused her, lifting her higher and lifting, and as if climbing the side of a volcano, the tension grew within her, excitement, dread, the coiling sensation so tight and fierce she didn't know why she didn't reach the peak, didn't know how he could draw the pleasure out longer.

But he did. And she rippled beneath him, hands clutched in his hair, her heart pounding so hard she couldn't catch her breath.

Then suddenly they'd reached the mouth of the volcano and everything was so hot and bright Ana felt dazzled by it all. Her body exploded, her insides like molten lava itself, and her hands fell to Lucio's shoulders, nails digging in for support.

She'd barely recovered from the exquisite sensation when Lucio lifted her in his arms, wrapped her legs around his hips, and leaning her against the rock, slowly buried himself inside her.

Ana gasped at the fullness of him, her body still so sensitive, and her muscles tightened helplessly.

With him buried deep, she pressed her face to his chest, her heart still racing. He felt so good. She loved the way he held her, and with him in her, she felt as if they were one person, joined forever.

"You're so hot," he whispered. "I've never felt you this hot."

She pressed a kiss to his lips. "I've never loved you this much."

Slowly, gently, he began to move, and slowly, gently he made love to her, and even though the rock pressed against her back and Lucio's shirt crushed her breasts, Ana had never enjoyed anything so much.

For long minutes they moved together, her legs wrapped around his waist, her arms around his neck, and it was like being part of the night, part of nature. The emotion inside Anabella was so strong, she couldn't imagine ever wanting more. Couldn't imagine life ever getting better than this.

And when Lucio couldn't hold back any longer, Ana surrendered, too, her body rippling and dancing around his.

Lucio didn't think he'd ever tire of holding Anabella, and he cradled her against him as their sated bodies cooled.

Tenderly he brushed Ana's long hair back from her face, her nape still damp, her lovely body naked in his arms.

"I'm going in the morning," he said quietly, holding her close against him. He felt her immediately stiffen but he didn't stop talking, and he didn't let her go. "I'm going with Victor," he continued matter of factly, "and I'll be gone a couple days. Two, maybe three. No more than three."

"You're leaving me here?"

He heard the shock in her voice. Angrily she pressed against his chest, trying to escape.

"I want you to stay here," he answered. "You'll be safe here. The others will look out for you."

Her fine features pinched. Her wide eyes were cloudy with hurt. "But why are you going with Victor? *Where* are you going with Victor?"

"To Jujuy."

"You're going to *Casa de Niños* without me!"

"I can travel faster without you."

He said it unapologetically and she shook her head, eyes flashing. "You said we'd do this together. You said we'd make this trip together—"

"You want to find Tomás, don't you?"

She didn't speak. But he knew her answer.

"Victor knows some people," he continued. "He has

some connections with people that could be dangerous, and I'm willing to take the risk, but I'm not willing to risk you.''

''I don't want you doing something dangerous. Maybe we should wait for Alonso. He said he'd be back in a couple weeks. It's not so long—''

''Come on, *negrita,* don't be a coward now. You know as well as I do that we can't wait. We're both worried about the child. We're both anxious to discover his whereabouts, know that he's safe.''

Ana slid out from beneath his arm, and scooped up her clothes. She pulled her knit top over her head and reached for her thong and gauze skirt.

Lucio saw the set of her mouth, the tears shimmering in her eyes. He leaned forward and pulled her back into his arms. ''*Negrita,* you said you'd trust me.''

She averted her head. ''We're supposed to be a team!''

''We are a team.''

''But a team doesn't leave half its members behind when the other half is walking into danger!''

He wanted to smile but didn't dare. She was already so angry, so hurt, and yet he was touched by her protest. She made him feel so much, and he liked the way she made him feel. No, he loved the way she made him feel and he'd never do anything to jeopardize Ana's well-being.

''We are a team,'' he repeated kindly, ''but it's not always completely equal, not an exact fifty fifty.''

''No, it's more like ninety to ten!'' she retorted.

''Not true. If you think about it, *flaca,* you've pretty much run the show in Mendoza. Our life has been shaped by you, your family, your needs.'' He saw her mouth open and he held up a hand. ''And I've accepted that, never regretted any of the choices I've made, but we're in my world now and I'm making the final decisions.''

''But I'm strong, Lucio. I'm smart. You don't have to leave me behind.''

Warmth filled him as her small proud chin lifted and her

green eyes pleaded with him, silently begging him not to leave her when she wanted to go as badly as she did.

She didn't know it, but she was truly his match, truly his mate, truly his better half. If she'd been born in Salta, in a family like his, she'd be an *amazona,* a *gaucha*—a female version of him.

Maybe another man would be overwhelmed by her spirit, her fire, her hot emotions, but he loved them. Each one of them. She was so alive, so much like nature all around them. She reminded him of the wind and the rain, the sun and the moon, and the fire within the earth which harbored lava and hot thermal springs.

He took her chin in his fingers. "We are like the *honero,*" he said, speaking of the little bird in Argentina that was just a bit bigger than the robin. "The female *honero* picks her mate based on the nest the male *honero* builds. The female is very choosy. She likes to be comfortable, but more importantly, she wants to be safe. She doesn't mate with the first male that comes along. No, she inspects each male's nest."

Ana's lips quivered. "You're telling me about a bird and nest building *now?*"

He suppressed the urge to laugh. She was so indignant, so furious with him still. "Yes. This is a good story. Listen." He gave her chin a little pinch. "The female *honero* wants only the best nest builder because that nest— her home—must protect her and the babies from the wind and the cold and predators that might prey on their young."

He lowered her chin and looked into her eyes. "You picked me, *carida,* because you know I am the best nest builder for you. You know no one else can give you the safety and the protection you need. You know—" he paused, lowered his head, brushed his lips across hers, "—no one else will ever love you as much as I do."

Ana tried to calm the wild, fierce beating of her heart. She'd hated the beginning of Lucio's story but by the end, her heart felt as if it'd burst.

"You *do* still love me," she whispered, fresh tears welling in her eyes.

"Of course. *Honeros, mi mujer, mi amor,* mate for life. I am yours for life. Just as you are mine." His head descended and he captured her lips in a long slow kiss that stole her breath, melted her resistance and made her crawl back into his arms and want to stay there forever.

"Trust me," he said, his body so warm against her, his arms so strong around her.

"I do."

"I will never desert you, never betray you, and never endanger you. Believe me, Ana. I will come for you, or send for you, as soon as I know something. As soon as I'm sure it's safe."

She nodded, tears thick in her throat, love flaming her heart. "Okay. You can go in the morning," she whispered, wrapping her arms around his neck. "But you have to make love to me again tonight first."

Lucio was gone two days. The first day seemed to last forever, and the second seemed nearly as long. Late afternoon on the second day she sat on a rock near the lake, her arms wrapped around her bent knees. The sun had dropped and the afternoon heat was giving way to cooler temperatures.

She knew by dusk she'd need her poncho again, knew that the cool would swiftly turn cold. There'd be another night with the others around the fire. Another night of quiet conversation punctuated with husky laughter. The gauchos worked hard during the day. At night they came together to relax, find companionship, let off steam with friends.

It was a simple life.

It was like nothing she'd ever known.

The sun dropped lower in the sky and Anabella looked up at the group of men arriving on horseback. They rode hard, white shirts blowing, billowing, their leather chaps flapping, black hats low on their heads.

One of the men rode straight to Ana. For a moment she

thought it was Lucio and climbed to her feet. But it wasn't Lucio. It was another gaucho.

She shaded her eyes to see him properly, and yet even then the sun glinted off of his head, radiating out in a stream of gold light. The gaucho was damp with perspiration and his thin cotton shirt clung to his chest, the faded fabric outlining the hard planes of muscles, the open neckline showing off the burnished copper of his skin.

Ana didn't know him but he reminded her of Lucio. Similar hard, carved features. His nose was a little thinner, his mouth not quite so generous. But there was a kindness about his eyes.

"Senora Cruz," the gaucho said, sliding off his horse. He was tall—not quite as tall as Lucio—but a good head taller than the rest of the gauchos. "You're to ride with me. We're to leave right away. Lucio wants you there by morning."

She glanced helplessly at the others. The gauchos at the fire didn't seem the least bit concerned. "We're going to travel all night?"

"It's not difficult," he answered carelessly.

She felt a wave of fear. How could she trust him? He didn't look hard, or cruel, but one never knew. "Just the two of us?"

"No, the others will ride with us." He nodded his head, indicating the two gauchos waiting by the lake. "Don't worry. You won't be alone with me."

"No. I'll be alone with three strange men."

His lips nearly curved. His dark eyes glinted. "Lucio said to remind you about the *honero*. He said to remind you that it was you who picked him."

Some of her unease faded. The *honero*. Argentina's savvy little nest builder. She almost smiled. Only Lucio would think to remind her of a little brown bird that mates for life. Only Lucio would remind her that she was his for life.

Her gaze met the gaucho's and the man smiled faintly. There was amusement in his dark eyes and the twist of his lips. "Don't worry. Lucio wouldn't send just anyone after you. You are his heart. He entrusted you to me because he knows I am nearly as fierce as he."

She stared unblinking into his dark eyes. "You must know him well."

"I should." He extended his hand to her. "I am Orlando Cruz, Lucio's younger brother. Which makes you my sister."

Lucio's brother. Her gaze continued to hold his and she wasn't sure if she should laugh or cry. Slowly she put her hand into his. She'd wanted to meet Lucio's family and now here was one. Trust Lucio to do introductions his way. "*Hola*, Orlando."

His hand wrapped around hers. Sure, hard, warm. "*Hola, benita* Anabella. Let's get your things. We must go."

They rode all night, Ana sitting in front of Orlando, half buried by the thick fleece of his saddle. She tried to sit tall and straight, keeping her distance, but sometime in the night, fatigue set in and her eyes closed.

It took Ana a moment to register that they had stopped moving and were no longer in motion. Everything had gone quiet.

She felt strong hands lift her and sleepily she opened her eyes. Ana blinked. *"Lucio?"*

He grinned as he set her on her feet. "No, you're not dreaming, *flaca*. You're here with me."

Not only was she with him, but it was no longer night. The rising sun lightened the sky, enhancing the cloudless blue. She glanced around, realizing they were in a small town, standing in front of a simple stone and plaster building. "What time is it?"

"A little after seven."

Suddenly she was very awake and she remembered why Lucio had left her, remembered why Lucio had sent for her. "You learned something about Tomás."

"I did." Lucio took the saddlebag from Orlando, and

with his arm around Ana's waist, walked her towards the building.

"So tell me!"

"You don't want coffee first? A bite to eat?"

"No." She clutched the front of his shirt. "Is he alive? Is he okay? Tell me, Lucio, that he's safe."

His long hair fell forward and he tucked thick strands behind his ear. "He is safe. But this is complicated. Maybe you should sit down first. Have something in your stomach—"

"No!" She wrapped her arms around his middle, holding him close. "Please, Lucio, you're scaring me. What happened to him? Where is he?"

Lucio's grip on her bag shifted and he opened the door to the small house. It was rather dim inside and Ana felt Lucio's hand press into the small of her back, propelling her forward.

Suddenly she stopped moving.

Afraid, Ana reached for his hand. *"Lucio."*

"I'm here."

She blinked hard and yet the two people standing in front of her didn't go away. A tall, broad-shouldered man with thick black hair standing next to a small boy.

"Good morning, Anabella."

She recognized the voice. She'd only heard it a couple times but she'd never forget the accent, or the cultured speech. "Alonso?"

"It's good to see you here," he said and as he smiled she noticed the narrow scar on his cheekbone. "We've been expecting you."

We've been expecting you? What did that mean?

She looked at Alonso and the child. Ana went hot. Cold. She began to tremble.

She looked again at the little boy. This time she saw only the little boy. *Tomás.*

Her lips parted. He wasn't a baby. He was boy with black hair. Light gold skin. Green eyes.

Green eyes.

Green eyes.

Ana couldn't see. Tears blinded her. She turned to Lucio, buried her face against his chest. She was shivering violently, shiver after shiver. *Please. Please. Please.*

It'd been a nightmare. And a dream. It'd been hell. Please God let it now be heaven.

"Anabella," Alonso was speaking again. "This is Tomás. He's five and he'd very much like to have a real bed, a real house, and a real mama and papa."

Ana's heart felt as if it'd burst. She turned her head, her cheek still pressed to Lucio's chest. *Let him still be there…let him still be there…Please God…*

She opened her eyes. He was still there. Lovely olive skin. Thick dark hair in dire need of a cut. A firm mouth that didn't smile much.

But it was his eyes that caught her, his eyes that made her hope.

His eyes made her believe.

"Ana," Lucio said, his deep voice husky with emotion. "We've found our son."

Her fingers found his, held tightly. She looked up at Lucio, not sure what to think, not sure how any of this came to be. "Is he really ours—"

"He's really ours."

"I don't mean biologically, I don't care if he's ours biologically, but is he ours? Can we adopt him? Can we take him home—"

"Ana," Lucio interrupted, "he's *ours.* Biologically ours. You were right all the time, *carida,* you did have a baby. This is our baby."

Ana felt as if she were being choked. It was hard to breathe, very hard to swallow. "How do you know?"

"We've done a DNA test," Alonso said. "The results came in last night."

"But you said last year…you said he couldn't be—"

"I was wrong." Alonso grimaced apologetically. "He

was so small that we miscalculated his age. The doctor working with us believed he was a year younger than your son would have been.''

Who was the 'we' Alonso was talking about? Who was the doctor that had seen Tomás?

Ana shook her head, unable to take it all in. She wanted desperately to go to Tomás, to wrap him in her arms, but he looked remote, detached from everybody and everything, and she didn't want to overwhelm him.

''Alonso hadn't really left the country,'' Lucio continued, hugging her closer to him. ''He was working with the government, trying to get the child legally returned to us, but he didn't want to meet with us until he had some definitive answers.''

She couldn't believe how calm Lucio was. Her own legs were shaking, her knees practically knocking. She felt hot and cold all over. ''When did you have the blood drawn for the DNA test?''

''In Mendoza, the day after I spoke to Alonso I stopped by Dr. Dominguez' office. He took the blood sample. And Alonso already had a blood sample from Tomás. They took one last year when they rescued him from *Casa de Niños*.''

She darted a look at Tomás who still looked quite grave, but perfectly unafraid. For a young child he had remarkable composure. ''You never said anything to me.''

Lucio's shoulders shifted. ''I didn't want to get your hopes up, and quite frankly, I didn't know what to believe, so I started an investigation of my own.''

She looked again at Tomás, at his small smile and she smiled herself despite the incredible knots of joy and pain.

She wanted her arms around him. She wanted to hug him close but was afraid if she touched him right now, she'd fall apart, was afraid the tears she'd been battling would start to fall and it'd frighten him. She had to think of him, think of all the things he must be going through.

Yet he stood so tall and he had such a strong little face, and such fierce dark eyes.

Like Lucio. Like his uncle Orlando. She smiled faintly. Like her own brothers, Dante and Tadeo.

"So what happens now?" she choked, tears not far off, feeling a surge of almost unbearable joy. Maybe she couldn't hug him yet, but there'd be hundreds of hugs later. And bubble baths and stories and trips to the playground at the park.

Alonso's hard expression gentled. "You meet with a couple officials later today, finish some paperwork, and you take your son home."

She swayed on her feet, dazed yet again, delighted a thousand times over. "That's it?"

"Not quite." Lucio hesitated. "Ana, before you get too excited, there's something else you must know. Tomás doesn't come alone."

Ana glanced from Lucio to Alonso. What did he mean? Was Tomás sick? Or had something bad happened? "Tell me he hasn't been hurt by someone."

"No, nothing quite like that, although he has been through a lot, shuffled from home to home and then orphanage to orphanage for the past four years."

Ana felt a lance of pain. To think Tomás had been through so much. She still had so many questions to ask, so much she needed to know, but now wasn't the time, not with Tomás standing stiff as a little soldier.

Lucio nodded at Alonso and Alonso made a movement, and slowly, very gently drew another little boy from behind him.

Ana gasped and felt Lucio's arm tighten around her. *Another child?*

Lucio smiled encouragingly at the small boy trying desperately to hide behind Alonso's powerful frame, but otherwise made no move towards the young child. "During the past year, as he settled into his new orphanage, Tomás adopted this fellow."

Lucio's voice was low, gentle, reassuring. "Tomás considers Tulio his brother. Tomás's quite protective of Tulio. Even Alonso will tell you how close the children are.''

No one said anything for a moment. Ana's heart pounded.

Lucio glanced at Anabella. ''I would not like to separate them.'' His dark eyes met hers and held. ''But I will not force the decision. The choice is yours.''

Was there even a choice? She wondered, as she saw how Tomás—*their* Tomás—stepped towards Tulio and took Tulio's small, plump hand in his.

Tomás had Ana's coloring, but Tulio was darker, more Indian with the straight thick black hair, large dark eyes, beautiful golden skin.

Tulio was just a toddler. He couldn't have been more than two, two and a half years, at the most. ''So we'd have two boys,'' she said softly.

Lucio's voice was hushed as well. ''I know it's a lot to decide now—''

''No. It's not too much. We'll take them both home, we *have* to.''

''I don't want you to do it out of obligation. I know until recently you'd never wanted to adopt, and I don't want to force this on you now when you're tired—''

''Stop.'' She gripped his forearm and shook her head. It was ridiculous, pointless, to even bring that old argument up now. ''There's no difference between the children. Tomás might be biologically ours, but he's a stranger to us, and we to him. There will be a huge adjustment regardless. And if he loves Tulio, they ought to remain together. They should come to us as brothers.''

''We don't have to make the decision now.''

But they did. She knew it, and he knew it, too.

She felt his gaze, felt his stillness. He didn't want to push her, or influence her. Lucio truly wanted what she wanted and Ana felt waves of love for him, waves of tenderness and need. He'd become a warrior for her. He'd become a prince. A vintner. A scholar.

''This will change everything,'' she said, glancing at the

boys with their small shoulders, their thin straight legs, their hands tightly gripped. They were facing an unknown future and they were so steadfast, so unflinching about it.

Her heart turned inside out. Children should never have to be so brave.

"It already has," Lucio answered.

Ana's eyes filled with tears. It was true. Just learning about Tomás changed everything. It wasn't just Lucio and Anabella anymore. It wasn't just about romance, lovemaking, passion. It was about family. It was about strength, love, courage, stability.

It was about hope.

And most of all it was about keeping faith even in the face of fear and uncertainty.

Ana sank to her knees, her trembling hands pressed to her thighs, and for a long moment she studied both boys' small faces, studied their solemn eyes, one pair dark, one pair green, and she smiled even as tears clung to her lashes. "*Hola*, Tomás and Tulio. I am Anabella Cruz. I am your mama."

Your opinion is important to us! Please take a few moments to share your thoughts with us about your experiences with Harlequin and Silhouette books. Your comments will be very useful in ensuring that we deliver books you love to read. *Please take a few minutes to complete the questionnaire, then send it to us at the address below.*

Send your completed questionnaires to:
Harlequin/Silhouette Reader Survey, P.O. Box 9046, Buffalo, NY 14269-9046

1. As you may know, there are many different lines under the Harlequin and Silhouette brands. Each of the lines is listed below. Please check the box that most represents your reading habit for each line.

Line	Currently read this line	Do not read this line	Not sure if I read this line
Harlequin American Romance	❏	❏	❏
Harlequin Duets	❏	❏	❏
Harlequin Romance	❏	❏	❏
Harlequin Historicals	❏	❏	❏
Harlequin Superromance	❏	❏	❏
Harlequin Intrigue	❏	❏	❏
Harlequin Presents	❏	❏	❏
Harlequin Temptation	❏	❏	❏
Harlequin Blaze	❏	❏	❏
Silhouette Special Edition	❏	❏	❏
Silhouette Romance	❏	❏	❏
Silhouette Intimate Moments	❏	❏	❏
Silhouette Desire	❏	❏	❏

2. Which of the following best describes why you bought *this book*? One answer only, please.

the picture on the cover	❏	the title	❏
the author	❏	the line is one I read often	❏
part of a miniseries	❏	saw an ad in another book	❏
saw an ad in a magazine/newsletter	❏	a friend told me about it	❏
I borrowed/was given this book	❏	other: _____	❏

3. Where did you buy *this book*? One answer only, please.

at Barnes & Noble	❏	at a grocery store	❏
at Waldenbooks	❏	at a drugstore	❏
at Borders	❏	on eHarlequin.com Web site	❏
at another bookstore	❏	from another Web site	❏
at Wal-Mart	❏	Harlequin/Silhouette Reader	❏
at Target	❏	Service/through the mail	
at Kmart	❏	used books from anywhere	❏
at another department store or mass merchandiser	❏	I borrowed/was given this book	❏

4. On average, how many Harlequin and Silhouette books do you buy at one time?

I buy _____ books at one time ❏
I rarely buy a book ❏

MRQ403HP-1A

5. How many times per month do you shop for any *Harlequin and/or Silhouette* books?
One answer only, please.

1 or more times a week	❑	a few times per year	❑
1 to 3 times per month	❑	less often than once a year	❑
1 to 2 times every 3 months	❑	never	❑

6. When you think of your ideal heroine, which *one* statement describes her the best?
One answer only, please.

She's a woman who is strong-willed	❑	She's a desirable woman	❑
She's a woman who is needed by others	❑	She's a powerful woman	❑
She's a woman who is taken care of	❑	She's a passionate woman	❑
She's an adventurous woman	❑	She's a sensitive woman	❑

7. The following statements describe types or genres of books that you may be interested in reading. Pick *up to 2 types* of books that you are most interested in.

I like to read about truly romantic relationships	❑
I like to read stories that are sexy romances	❑
I like to read romantic comedies	❑
I like to read a romantic mystery/suspense	❑
I like to read about romantic adventures	❑
I like to read romance stories that involve family	❑
I like to read about a romance in times or places that I have never seen	❑
Other: _____	❑

The following questions help us to group your answers with those readers who are similar to you. Your answers will remain confidential.

8. Please record your year of birth below.
    19 _____

9. What is your marital status?
    single ❑   married ❑   common-law ❑   widowed ❑
    divorced/separated ❑

10. Do you have children 18 years of age or younger currently living at home?
    yes ❑   no ❑

11. Which of the following best describes your employment status?
    employed full-time or part-time ❑   homemaker ❑   student ❑
    retired ❑   unemployed ❑

12. Do you have access to the Internet from either home or work?
    yes ❑   no ❑

13. Have you ever visited eHarlequin.com?
    yes ❑   no ❑

14. What state do you live in?
    _____

15. Are you a member of Harlequin/Silhouette Reader Service?
    yes ❑   Account # _____   no ❑   MRQ403HP-1B